P9-DML-779

THE BEST PLAYS FROM THE STRAWBERRY ONE-ACT FESTIVAL

Dear Andrea —
Thanks for being
part of it!
Always,
Michele Leigh

THE BEST PLAYS FROM THE STRAWBERRY ONE-ACT FESTIVAL

Volume Five

Compiled by Van Dirk Fisher

iUniverse, Inc.
New York Bloomington Shanghai

The Best Plays From The Strawberry One-Act Festival
Volume Five

Copyright © 2008 by Van Dirk Fisher

All rights reserved. No part of this book may be used or reproduced by any means, graphic, electronic, or mechanical, including photocopying, recording, taping or by any information storage retrieval system without the written permission of the publisher except in the case of brief quotations embodied in critical articles and reviews.

iUniverse
1663 Liberty Drive
Bloomington, IN 47403
www.iuniverse.com
1-800-Authors (1-800-288-4677)

Because of the dynamic nature of the Internet, any Web addresses or links contained in this book may have changed since publication and may no longer be valid.

This is a work of fiction. All of the characters, names, incidents, organizations, and dialogue in this novel are either the products of the author's imagination or are used fictitiously.

ISBN: 978-0-595-51323-9 (pbk)
ISBN: 978-0-595-61849-1 (ebk)

Printed in the United States of America

CAUTION: Professionals and amateurs are hereby warned that *Cold April, Reunion, Fighting Fires, Jack, Marked, Always Anastasia, This Quiet House* and *What Cheer, Iowa* are subject to a royalty. They are fully protected under the copyright laws of the United States of America, the British Commonwealth, including Canada, and all other countries of the Copyright Union. All rights, including professional, amateur, motion pictures, recitation, lecturing, public reading, radio broadcasting, television, and the rights of translation into foreign languages are strictly reserved. In its present form the play is dedicated to the reading public only.

The amateur live stage performance rights to *Cold April, Reunion, Fighting Fires, Jack, Marked, Always Anastasia, This Quiet House* and *What Cheer, Iowa* are controlled exclusively by The Riant Theatre and The Black Experimental Theatre, Inc., and royalty arrangements and licenses must be secured well in advance of presentation. PLEASE NOTE that amateur royalty fees are set upon application in accordance with your producing circumstances. When applying for a royalty quotation and license please give us the number of performances intended, dates of production, your seating capacity and admission fee. Royalties are payable one week before the opening performance of the play to The Riant Theatre, P.O. Box 1902, New York, NY 10013.

Royalty of the required amount must be paid whether the play is presented for charity or gain and whether or not admission is charged.

Stock royalty quoted on application to The Riant Theatre.

For all other rights than those stipulated above, apply to The Riant Theatre, P.O. Box 1902, New York, NY 10013 or TheRiantTheatre@aol.com.

Particular emphasis is laid on the question of amateur or professional readings, permission and terms for which must be secured in writing from The Riant Theatre.

Copying from this book in whole or in part is strictly forbidden by law, and the right of performance is not transferable.

Whenever the play is produced the following notice must appear on all programs, printing and advertising for the play: "Produced by special arrangement with The Riant Theatre."

Due authorship credit must be given on all programs, printing and advertising for the play.

No one shall commit or authorize any act or omission by which the copyright of, or the right to copyright, this play may be impaired.

No one shall make any changes in this play for the purpose of production.

Publication of this play does not imply availability for performance. Both amateurs and professionals considering a production are *strongly* advised in their own interests to apply to The Riant Theatre for written permission before starting rehearsals, advertising, or booking a theatre.

No part of this book may be reproduced, stored in a retrieval system, or transmitted in any form, by any means, now known or yet to be invented, including mechanical, electronic, photocopying, recording, videotaping, or otherwise, without the prior written permission of The Riant Theatre.

This anthology as well as Volume 1 through Volume 4 may be purchased online at www. therianttheatre.com, and wherever books are sold.

CONTENTS

▼

THE
RIANT
THEATRE

www.TheRiantTheatre.com

Welcome to the 5th Volume of the Best Plays From The Strawberry One-Act Festival. **The Strawberry One-Act Festival**, which began in 1995 in New York City, is the brainchild of The Riant Theatre's Artistic Director, Van Dirk Fisher. The festival is a play competition in which the audience and the theatre's judges cast their votes to select the best play of the season.

Twice a year, hundreds of plays from across the country are submitted for the competition, of which 50 are chosen to compete. Plays move from the 1st round to the semi-finals and then the finals. The playwright of the winning play receives a grant and the opportunity to have a full-length play developed by the Riant. In addition, awards are given out for Best Director, Best Actor and Best Actress.

During the Winter Strawberry One-Act Festival (2007), the Riant brought the festival to a worldwide audience by making performances available for viewing online at www.therianttheatre.com/video. During the festival, viewers were able to visit the site, watch the plays online, and cast their votes for best play, director, actor and actress. We are very excited about this new technology and how it enables us to give our playwrights and artists additional exposure—along with our year-round online features that include interviews with our playwrights, directors and actors.

The Strawberry One-Act Festival is a wonderful opportunity for the audience and the industry alike to see some of the best talent in the nation. Every performance features four dynamic one-act plays. There's always a lot of buzz surrounding each performance as artists converge and network on future projects. Several of the playwrights whose plays are featured in the festival have written for the literary world, as well as for television and film. "We are very fortunate to be able to fulfill our mission, which is to discover and develop talent and playwrights for the stage," says Mr. Fisher. "We are very proud of this accomplishment, but the work doesn't stop there. Competition aside, everyone's a winner in the festival, because several actors, directors and playwrights are chosen to work on future projects at the Riant."

The Strawberry One-Act Festival features 10 Series of plays in Round I. Each Series consists of four one-act plays of various lengths, with 30 minutes being the maximum running time. Round I of the competition runs for approximately 10 days, with shows at 7pm and 9pm. In Round I of the competition, each play is performed over two consecutive days. After viewing a series, the audience fills out their voting ballots and is asked to select the two plays that they like the best, as well as the best director, actor and actress. After the second day of performances in a series, the votes are tallied and the two plays with the most points move on to the Semi-Finals of the competition.

The Semi-Finals follow with five Series of plays, consisting of five plays for each series competing against each other. In the Semi-Finals, each play is presented over two days. After each day of performances, the audience fills out their ballots and selects the two plays that they like the best. After the second day of performances, the votes are tallied and the play with the most votes moves on to the Finals. A Wild Night is also presented, in which eight plays that didn't make it to the Semi-Finals are given another chance to compete for a spot in the Finals. The eight plays chosen for the Wild Night are decided by the artistic director, Van Dirk Fisher.

The Finals consists of seven plays. The judges are the audience, whose votes count for 40% of the vote, the playwrights of the plays, and the artistic director, Van Dirk Fisher, whose votes count for 60% of the vote.

During the Summer 2007 Festival, the audience's votes—as well as those of the playwrights in attendance—selected *REUNION* by Brian Podnos as the Best Play of the Season. The winner of the Winter 2008 Festival was *COLD APRIL* by John P. McEneny. As winner of the festival, the playwright has the opportunity to present a full-length play or a new play, to be considered for development by the Riant.

Each of the plays featured in this volume of the literary anthology were performed in The Strawberry One-Act Festival during the Summer 2007 Festival or the Winter 2008 Festival.

The first play in our anthology is *COLD APRIL* by John P. McEneny. It's a very powerful and moving drama set in Rawanda in 1994, in the Girl's Dormitory of the St. Maria Goretti Secondary School, in which a thirteen year old girl refuses to hand over her friends to the Hutu rebels. The innocence of the young girls pitted against the brutal force of the rebels in Rawanda is a remarkable testimony to the unifying strength of love over the inhumanity of man against man. The genocide of people is an act that no one should have to witness and something the world should not turn a blind eye upon, for it is an injustice that should haunt our hearts and minds and stir us to action to end such atrocities before they hit home and remind us that history often repeats itself. This timely play was a reminder to all who witnessed it, and by the curtain's end there was not a dry eye in the house.

Marc Anthony said in Julius Ceasar, "The evil that men do lives after them." Well in *REUNION* by Brian Podnos, the demons of the past are brought to light when a father and son are forced to face the problems in their relationship. Peter, the son, who's recently been released from rehab, returns home to confront his father upon learning of his mother's untimely demised. The jealousies that have eroded the father's love for his son, prevents him from notifying his son of his mother's illness. Therefore, robbing the son of the opportunity to say goodbye to his mother. Can this strained relationship be healed and will the reunion enable them to move forward or will the coffin be nailed shut as the final blow is struck? Find out in this award winning drama about love and hate.

The theme "relationships between father and son" is revisited in *FIGHTING FIRES* by Von H. Washington, Sr., with some surprising results, as a young man on the eve of his 18th birthday, kidnaps his absentee father and demands the attention he believes was owed him during his developmental years. The method in which this play unfolds is very dramatic with an unnerving climax. This play is a shout out and a wake up call to every deadbeat dad, who thinks depositing his seed ends his responsibility to the life he breeds. Think again! The child you leave behind may be the one who some day determines your fate.

If we could control our fate who would choose to be poor? And if we could turn our lives around and make the lives of our loved ones easier and prosperous, who would pass up the opportunity? Well, no one I can think of off hand. The desire of a child to please his parents and the longing for approval is a common trait innate in many of us. Daren Taylor puts a spiritual spin on a familiar fairy tale *Jack In The Beanstalk* with his play *JACK*. Here we find Jack living in poverty with his mother and is blessed when he buys magic seeds from a mysterious figure and climbs an enchanted beanstalk and believes that he's seen God. Who will believe him? His testimony is a true test for all believers that there is a God and the belief that God answers prayers. *JACK* questions our moral compass in a world where greed and corruption abounds and innocence and altruism is a rare commodity that's hardly cherished.

In such a world, in time, one can easily lose one's scruples and mind. Then all one would have to depend on is family to take care of us in our old age and time of need. Such is the case of Lana in Cassandra Lewis' *MARKED*, in which Lana's son, Francis is forced to visit his mother to warn her to take her medication or fear losing her independence and face being placed in an institution. *MARKED* is a wonderful dark comedy that explores the connection between love, insanity and social responsibility.

But what about the marital responsibility between husband and wife? Are there rules that should be followed or is mankind simply insane to think that we mortal mammals are capable of fidelity? In *ALWAYS, ANASTASIA* by Michele Leigh, a disillusioned cop on the verge of a nervous breakdown believes that he is being tormented by a narcissistic psychopath, but the demons that haunt him lie deeper than his soul, and only if the truth is revealed can the spirits that haunt him rest in peace. I loved this mystery and I'm sure you will too.

We all have the burning desire to get to bottom of the truth. But what if the truth is so scorching and painful to the eye that we must rid it from our sight in order to breathe—to live and survive? In *THIS QUIET HOUSE* by Toby Levin, a stepmother's desire to have a son catches fire in an unspeakable way. When her husband's inability to quench her thirst falls short, she reaches out to his strappingly handsome and virile son to help her *lose her breath*, a catch phrase coined by Beyoncé in one of her hit songs. The barn is the perfect place where the horses are kept. The setting is perfect with hay everywhere to serve as the welcoming bed. The scent in the air is strong and sweet. The quiet night suggests the timing is just right. A cool breeze even manages to offer some temporary relief, but what the stepmother longs for in this titillating tale is something more lasting, throbbing and exhilaratingly satisfying. It's going to be a bumpy ride so sit back and enjoy this page turning drama about love and lust.

Just when you thought things couldn't get any crazier and you've had a moment to cool off with a tall glass of iced tea, Jeff Belanger has topped things off with his zany hilarious play *WHAT CHEER, IOWA*, where tempers flare and sanity is on the line as five people struggle against the gargantuan pressure of waiting to find out if their cars passed their annual inspection. Zach Harvey received the Best Actor Award for his performance as James in this play and Sean Kenealy picked up the Best Director Award. If we could all be so lucky. This play was a true crowd pleaser.

I hope that you enjoy these wonderful plays as much as I have and several audiences that have graced the Strawberry One-Act Festival. To read some other outstanding plays pick up a copy of Volume 1 through 4. I feel honored and blessed to have had the opportunity to see these plays performed on stage and even more wonderful to be able to reread them whenever I choose to be entertained or inspired. Their universal themes and artistry is an inspiration to all and I thank them for sharing their talents and generosity of spirit. Both young and old veterans of theatre have graced the Riant Theatre's stages with their work, from community theatres to Broadway, from television to movie cinema, the common thread they all possess is a passion and love for theatre and touching peoples lives.

Enjoy! And remember if you're ever in New York City during the month of February, July or August come check out the Strawberry One-Act Festival and know that you are always—Welcome! Welcome! Welcome!

Van Dirk Fisher
Founder & Artistic Director
The Riant Theatre
P.O. Box 1902
New York, NY 10013
therianttheatre@aol.com

Join our fan club on MySpace at www.myspace.com/the1toknownow or www.myspace.com/strawberryoneactfestival. To hear some great music go to www.cdbaby.com/cd/toejambeats or www.myspace.com/toejambeats419 or www.myspace.com/lovingyouthemusical

*Sean Phillips as The Man in COLD APRIL by John P. McEneny
in The Riant Theatre's Strawberry One-Act Festival Winter 2008
at The American Theater of Actors in NYC*

COLD APRIL
By John P. McEneny

John P. McEneny was born and raised in Albany, NY and is the oldest son of John and Barbara McEneny. He runs the acclaimed drama program at William Alexander Middle School 51 in Park Slope, Brooklyn. With his lovely sister, Rachel, he created Piper Theatre Productions, which produces free Shakespearean productions at the Old Stone House in J. J. Byrne Park. He has directed over fifty plays and written dozens of youth plays including: *Mayla the Monkey Girl, The Midnight Circus, Grosse Isle, Shema,* and *The Puppet Children.* His play about the influenza epidemic of 1918, *The Grippe of October,* will be traveling to the Gordonstoun School in Scotland this April. He has an MA from NYU in Theatre in Education.

Cold April made its New York City debut on February 15, 2008 at the American Theatre of Actors. It was the winner of The Riant Theatre's Winter 2008 Strawberry One-Act Festival with the following cast in order of appearance:

ASURA, 13, Tutsi	Krysta Gonzalez
MOSI, 14, Hutu	Erica McLaughlin
KHATITI, 14, Tutsi	Jessica Porter
LAYLA, 13, Tutsi	Maggie Thompson
LULA, 13, Tutsi	Chloe Briggs
SALA, 13, Hutu	Chiara DeBlasio
MAN, 30, Hutu	Sean Phillips

The play was directed by John P. McEneny
Costumes designed by Celeste Hines

Cold April is inspired by the true story of the girls of St. Maria Goretti School in Muramba who stood up to the Hutu militia and refused to hand over their Tutsi classmates. They were all slaughtered.

Scene 1

April 1994, 7:30 p.m. St. Maria Goretti School in Muramba. The dormitory is a very clean, if slightly run down building. There is a crucifix across over the door and perhaps a picture of Maria Goretti, the Italian child saint who was canonized in 1950 for forgiving the man who raped and killed her. The sun is setting. The radio is playing a hazy French song. Asura, 14, a tall skittish girl enters. She locks the door behind her. She runs to her window, searching for someone that never comes. She takes a deep breath and sits, defeated. She turns off the radio. She then goes to the door to make sure it is locked. She then goes to the radio and turns it on again and switches from the music to the news.

RADIO: *(male voice)* Band together. Take back the power that was taken by the long necked roaches. Take back what is yours. Take back what was taken from your ancestors. Brothers will meet at East Wind Road at thirteen hundred hours and—(*Asura turns off the radio. She hides it. A knock on the door. Asura flinches.*)

ASURA: Khatitti? Is that you?

MOSI: Asura! It's just us. (*Asura opens the door. The girls enter and are wearing school uniforms. They are returning from the* lower school *dormitory. They are tired. Sala takes off her shoes. Lula flops down on her bed. Layla takes out her journal.*)

KHATITI: I'm exhausted. I never thought the little ones would get to bed. Asura, could you start a pot of coffee?

ASURA: I don't think there's any left. I looked in the kitchen this morning. There might be some tea.

LAYLA: My mother had seven children. And no aunties to help. S'no wonder she sent us away. I don't know how she did it.

ASURA: Did you lock the door by the front gate?

MOSI: It's not going to keep anyone out, Asura.

ASURA: Did you lock up the doors? Where is Mandani?

KHATITI: Mandani is going watch over them tonight. Make sure they don't get out of bed. It's her turn. Asura, try to get some rest. You haven't slept for days.

ASURA: All I asked is if you locked the door.

KHATITI: Don't be cheek. I'm not dealing with you tonight. Not tonight.

LULA: Yes. It's locked. Let's listen to the radio.

ASURA: No.

LAYLA: Oh please, Asura.

ASURA: I'm not listening. I hate the radio.

LULA: You hate <u>Radio Télévision Libre des Mille Collines</u>. There are other stations.

MOSI: Maybe I want to hear what they say. I want to hear the news.

ASURA: You know what they're saying. You know what he says.

MOSI: It can't hurt to listen.

ASURA: Yes it can. It's nothing but screaming and hate language; calling for the annihilation of all Tutsis. They're calling us names like "cockroaches" or "long necked slugs." They're calling my people this.

MOSI: Asura, I want to hear the radio. We want to hear the radio. You're being irrational just because you're scared.

ASURA: Mosi, it's nothing but hate speech. They're inciting violence. They're encouraging these men to pick up machetes.

MOSI: Machetes are cheaper than guns.

KHATITI: Shut up. You'll scare the little ones.

MOSI: They're asleep. I want to hear news from the Interahamwe.

ASURA: Thugs. Stupid violent thugs. Don't turn on the radio. I really can't bear it.

MOSI: No.

ASURA: We need to save the batteries. We don't know how long Miss Duvall will be gone.

MOSI: She's not coming back.

ASURA: Miss Duvall said she'd be back.

MOSI: Don't you understand what's going on? The Tutsis have murdered the president.

ASURA: They don't know that.

MOSI: Habyariman was murdered. And <u>Cyprien Ntaryamira</u> is dead. The Hutu president of Burundi is dead. Both presidents. People are trying to figure out how this happened and you know they're going to find it'll be some kind of Tutsi.

ASURA: It was a plane crash. And they haven't determined how it crashed. No one can conclude it was a Tutsi terrorist.

MOSI: His private plane was shot down. We need more details and the radio is only one attempting to give us answers.

ASURA: RTLM Radio is propaganda. You sound like a peasant listening to such hatred. Are you hearing what they're saying? It's not news at RTLM. They have an agenda to wipe out all Tutsis.

LAYLA: They're just words. Why are you fighting so? Let it be. It's late.

LULA: Maybe there will be some music later on. Maybe Aimé Murefu?

LAYLA: I love him. He's brilliant. Boshoshu sent me a tape in his last care package. He's got magic fingers.

LULA: Aimé Murefu or Boshoshu?

LAYLA: *(teasing)* Don't be coarse.

ASURA: Whose Boshoshu?

LULA: No, don't tease me. I'm serious. They're going to tease me.

LAYLA: Boshoshu is her boyfriend. They would sit for hours talking of music before Mother sent us to St. Maria Goretti's. She wanted to get Lula away from Boshoshu.

LULA: That's not true. She wanted us to be educated. Educated by Belgian Catholics.

LAYLA: Educated away from Boshoshu. Poor Lula cried like a sappy thing on the bus, all the way over to Muramba. (*Layla imitates a crying Lula.*) "Boshoshu is going to forget me … Mother can't keep us apart … Boshooooshu-"

LULA: Mother wants us to marry some French speaking educated men. I'm too young to be married anyhow.

KHATITI: Some girls are as young as eight when they get married.

LAYLA: That's only in the eastern provinces. They're backwards.

SALA: Someone is always thinking of marriage for girls. From the time you're born they're already deciding what man's right for you. What if a girl doesn't want to get married? Miss Duvall isn't married.

LAYLA: And who would want to marry her anyhow?

SALA: I think she's pretty if she didn't wear glasses all the time.

KHATITI: (*teasing*) Careful, people might accuse you of being an educated girl! And then no one will want to marry you.

SALA: Good.

LULA: I want to be educated and married. And Boshoshu would understand but my mother is thick and stupid.

MOSI: What was wrong with Boshoshu? Why didn't your mother want him around you?

LULA: I don't know.

MOSI: Was he older?

LULA: He was fifteen.

MOSI: Was he rude to your family?

LULA: No. Boshoshu was always appropriate.

MOSI: Did he drink?

LULA: No.

MOSI: Was he lazy? Did he refuse to help his father in the fields?

LULA: No.

MOSI: So then he was a Hutu? (*Lula doesn't answer. Layla turns away and looks disgusted at Mosi.*) Was he born into a Hutu family? Did he have Hutu blood? A heavy Hutu head?

LAYLA: That doesn't mean anything. Our whole neighborhood had Hutu's in it. They were our neighbors.

MOSI: You mean servants?

LAYLA: I didn't say servants.

MOSI: Then why couldn't Lula date a nice well spoken Hutu boy?

LAYLA: She didn't say that. You're twisting our words to fit your …

MOSI: My what?

LAYLA: Your politics. The way you think the world is.

MOSI: Open your eyes. Your Tutsi eyes have never even seen oppression.

ASURA: They're going to come here soon. They're to inspect all the schools.

LULA: We're fine to be, Asura. Miss Duvall has gone to the U.N. quarters. She wouldn't leave us alone if she was afraid for our safety.

SALA: Maybe they won't let her come get us.

ASURA: The rest of the teachers left. They left us alone. A whole school of girls alone.

LULA: But Miss Duvall stayed with us. She's only been gone for a few days. They'll listen to her. She's white.

ASURA: She's Belgian. It's not like she's an American.

LAYLA: Stop being so pessimistic, Asura. I can't make you less afraid.

ASURA: But the Kinyarwanda could be in the hills, just a few kilometers from the dormitory. They might kill us. *(She runs to the window; searching.)*

SALA: The Kinyarwanda are jobless peasants with too much time on their hands.

MOSI: And why do you think that is, Sala? Why do you think the Hutus are the peasantry? Who has held the power for the past thirty years?

ASURA: So the Hutus have the right to lash out? They have the right to kill their neighbors? Because they're angry?

MOSI: No. Well yes. I mean no. They don't have a right to kill. But they have a right to feel something.

ASURA: I get angry too. You don't see me killing anyone.

MOSI: It's not that they're angry, Asura. Violence doesn't come from anger, it comes from something else. It's something bigger than just a feeling. It's an overwhelming sense of injustice.

ASURA: The world will never be fair.

MOSI: But sometimes it should.

ASURA: But it's not. And you're a girl and you know that. And you have a rich uncle and go to a school. You should be happy with your fortune.

MOSI: I know.

SALA: You should be grateful.

MOSI: I am. It's just that I know that feeling. That scratching at your gut. When I was still in Butari, before my Uncle sent me here, my mother, my baby brother, and I lived on a coffee farm. And mother had saved all month to buy this white cotton from Kubye. It had been a miserable season with my father's death and the constant draught on the farm. I was sad often but I never complained or sighed. And then one night, as if my mother could read my thoughts, she came to my mat and called me her "good daughter." (*She takes a pause.*) She promised me a new dress and I hugged her. With that promise I knew she loved me and she knew how sad I had been and how much I had been through. This was before she got sick. The next morning we traveled nearly sixteen kilometers with my brother on my back to buy the cotton. And then when we got it home and she spent the whole week stitching together the cool fabric. And when she was done, she called me in from the road and there standing on the table was my little brother wearing a brand new cotton shirt and pants. He was smiling broadly at me with his giant white teeth like my father's. And I felt so hot. It was so unfair. I was such a good daughter. I took almost a year from my schooling so that I could help Mother after Papa died. I was obedient and quiet. I had worked so hard tending to Honor and the farm. And then something just woke up inside of me at that moment and I took my hand and slapped my brother's face. Hard. Harsh. Really hard. (*Pause. Asura turns away, vehemently disagreeing with Mosi. She crosses to the window searching for someone.*)

I would have done it again, if my mother had not screamed at me. And my violent act surprised me. I mean I loved my brother. I love Honor. I sang to him each morning. He is named for my father. I promised to always care for him. And yet there was something very strong inside me that needed to make it right, to make it just, to make it fair, even if that meant I had to hurt my brother. I don't know. (*Pause.*) Maybe it was more about doing it in front of my mother. Knowing that me, "the good daughter", could hurt someone. Could hurt her.

SALA: I would not hurt anyone.

MOSI: I think you would. I think we all would. I think we all have that potential inside of us.

ASURA: I think you're wrong, Mosi. I would never hurt anyone.

MOSI: Maybe because you're privileged Tutsi you feel that way.

ASURA: I have Hutu relatives. My great grandmother was a Hutu.

MOSI: But you're a Tutsi; racially superior.

ASURA: That's not fair.

MOSI: You could never understand the years of oppression that lay inside of us.

LAYLA: I don't like politics. Where is this getting us? Why are we fighting with each other?

MOSI: You don't like politics because you're a pampered rich girl who thinks you're life should not be affected by the suffering of others.

LAYLA: That's not true.

MOSI: I bet your Hutu boyfriend, Boshoshu, likes politics. I bet when you left, he sat by his tape player listening to Aimé Murefu play his weird sad songs just so long. And then he began thinking of his poor Lula sent away to a Catholic boarding school so that she wouldn't be tempted to be with a dirty Hutu boy like himself. And then maybe he would get tired of hearing these sad songs that he shared with you. And then he'd try to get an apprenticeship somewhere, but who is going to hire some low class Hutu boy? And he'd switch over to RTLM free Radio, and he'd hear Georges Ruggiu talking about how it was now time for the Hutus to rise up. Maybe Boshoshu would make right this world. Maybe he'd stop feeling sorry for himself. Maybe he'd become a soldier and join the guerilla forces to fight the Rwandan Patriotic Front.

LAYLA: Boshoshu is no soldier. He's a boy. He's just turned fifteen.

MOSI: Don't be naïve. Armies are filled with boys.

LAYLA: He's not a soldier.

MOSI: Then he's a mercenary, or a patriot, or a gang member. What's the difference? He'll do what he's told.

LULA: He doesn't like politics.

MOSI: No but he likes his Hutu family and friends. And if want to keep their respect and love, he might just have to join up with the rest of the militia.

LULA: *(she begins to cry)* And do what? Kill Tutsi's like me and my sister? He's to forget all and just come kill me?

MOSI: No. I mean … Lula. I didn't mean to make you cry.

LULA: And it's because of his weak Hutu bloodlines that he'll just snap and follow along with a murderous mob?

MOSI: I don't know, Lula.

KHATITI: Stop trying to scare her. Mosi, I'm a Hutu just like you and I know my family would never resort to violence. These are mad days for all of us. We're just teenagers at a convent secondary school. It's not doing any of us any good to be moping about with rumors. Miss Duvall told us to stay here in the East House and stay put. She'll come back with more information.

MOSI: Will she? Or have they killed her too.

KHATITI: They wouldn't kill a Westerner.

MOSI: I think thugs would kill anyone.

LAYLA: You mean a Hutu thug?

MOSI: I mean any thug.

ASURA: Do you hear that? Someone is walking on the cement. *(All are suddenly silent. A slight scraping sound is heard. The world stops. No one moves.)*

The men are here.

MOSI: Quiet.

LULA: Maybe it's the U.N. Soldiers.

KHATITI: Maybe it's Miss Duvall with troops to save us. Or take us to a safe house until our parents can get to us.

LAYLA: This is a safe house. They're not going to attack schools. We're just children. They're not going to kill children.

KHATITI: Do they have guns?

ASURA: Don't make a sound.

MALE VOICE: *(From a distance, barely audible, getting closer, perhaps louder.)* Those that stand together are those who fight. Those that stand together are those that fight. The Cockroaches must be terminated as one would stamp out a bug in your kitchen. Fifty years of oppression are over now, my brothers. You need to take their tall lanky frames and knock off their heads for all Hutu sons. Their future is dependent on your hands. Those that stand together are those who fight. Those that stand together are those that fight.

MOSI: It's the Interahamwe. They've come for us. *(Asura runs to the window, searching for someone.)*

MALE VOICE: Hutu, daughters of noble warriors, we come. Open your doors to us. Show us the Tutsis. Send out the Cockroaches.

ASURA: Quiet. Lula, stop crying.

MALE VOICE: No locks will keep us out. *(He knocks on the door.)*

KHATITI: Open the door.

LAYLA: No.

MALE VOICE: There is no place to hide. I see your movement in the shadows, let me in. I promise you that your causes will be much worse if you resist. *(Mosi opens the door. The soldier walks in. He is wearing shorts & a tee shirt open at the chest. He has a machete in his belt.)* You need to come out now.

MOSI: Are you alone?

MAN: My brothers from the Interhamwe will be here in moments. They are rising from the hills.

MOSI: I heard nothing.

MAN: We are not walking afraid anymore. We creep up on no one. You'll hear us all soon enough. Little girl, are you a cockroach?

MOSI: What do you mean?

MAN: Are you of Hutu blood?

MOSI: We are girls at St. Maria Goretti Secondary School. I am Mosi, the head girl. We have been on our own for the past four days since Miss Duvall went to the UN headquarters.

MAN: My list says that there are Tutsis at this school.

MOSI: There are no Tutsi here.

MAN: Do the nuns teach you to lie? I have the occupancy list from the Impuzamugambi.

MOSI: Please leave us be. We've done you no harm. These girls are no older than 13. We take care of the younger girls while Miss Duvall is gone. We just got them to sleep.

MAN: My brothers will take care of them. Why do you hide? Why is your door locked?

MOSI: The radio speaks of violence.

MAN: Yes, it does. We've got to rid our state of Tutsi vermin.

MOSI: Please, you need to leave us alone. We are just schoolgirls. We are not political animals. We take academic subjects here; Economics, French, English, sums, and history. We're taught to say prayers each night before we go to bed. We lead very quiet and simple lives. And someday we will be farmer's wives.

MAN: I'm not here to hurt my fellow Hutu. I'm here to kill the cockroaches.

MOSI: You make them sound like they're not human.

MAN: They're not.

MOSI: Then what are they?

MAN: We have been oppressed by these cockroaches our entire lives, little girl. Perhaps you'd have a dream greater than being a poor farmer's wife if these Tutsis didn't control everything. Maybe greater things are promised us. Maybe we should be living in the fine houses, drinking the fine wines, and driving the cars. Why should they have all the power and we die as poor and weak as our grandfathers? This is our time, girl. If you have read your history books, then you'd know that like all revolutions there is a time ... a time for the oppressed to rise up and take action. Now is our time for our bullets to show the rage that has been silent until now.

MOSI: You sound like the radio.

MAN: I sound like a man with a backbone. I sound like a Hutu with a voice to be heard.

MOSI: We are Hutu. Leave us be.

MAN: Liar. I have the list. Hold on. *(He pulls out a well worn notebook page from his back pocket. It is covered in blood. The girls react.)* Layla and Lula Gasana, 13. Daughters of General John Gasana. Asura Bundari, 13. Daughter of Sila and Gomair Bundari. Marie Mungu, 12. Daughter of-

MOSI: Stop. Those girls aren't here anymore. Miss Duvall took them to the UN. You'll have to talk to her when she gets back.

MAN: Your Miss Duvall isn't coming back. The UN has taken away all the westerners. She's probably back in France on her fat white ass. This is Africa. No one is going to take care of Africa except Africans.

MOSI: You're making my friends cry. Can you not see what is in front of you? How did you become this way?

MAN: I am lucky to live in this time to finally see justice.

MOSI: No, I mean, weren't you once a boy? A child. Can you understand how helpless we are? We are just children.

MAN: There is no childhood in Rwanda. There is nothing but hardship. I watched both my mother and father die of AIDS. I watched them vomit to death, begging to die, suffering in their own sweat. I watched my sister sold into slavery. The morning they took her, I begged the police to stop them. I begged my neighbors for help. I begged the priest to intervene. And no one would help a skinny Hutu boy. I ran after that white van for hours, crying hot tears, sobbing, stopping only until my legs would no longer hold out. No one would help me. There was no fine school for me to be sent to. I was no Tutsi born boy of privilege. There is no childhood in Rwanda. There is no childhood for me.

MOSI: I lost my parents too. My father died four years ago and my mother last year. My uncle sent me here when she got sick.

MAN: Where are you from?

MOSI: Buyumba originally and then Butari. My uncle and brother still live there.

MAN: And what is your name?

MOSI: Mosi. What is yours?

MAN: I'm not here to kill you, Mosi. Tell your friends to stand up. *(Layla, Sala, Asura, Khatiti stand up. Lula remains on the floor trembling.)* I said stand up.

LAYLA: She's frightened.

MAN: Why? Because she is a Tutsi? She should be frightened.

LAYLA: Lula, stand by me. Hold my hand. *(The man walks over to LULA and looks at his list again.)*

MAN: My friends will be here soon. We have the rest of the school to search and then we're moving into the town. Mosi, be a good sister and tell me which of these girls are Tutsis. I don't have a Mosi on my list, I won't hurt you.

MOSI: These are my friends.

MAN: There are Tutsis on my list, and there are Tutsis in this room and they will be taken outside and killed. Tell me which ones are to come with me and I'll let you be.

MOSI: I have known these girls for over two years, they are good …

MAN: Some of them are Tutsis and they have oppressed you and your people for decades. Hand them over now or I will kill all of you. *(He is hysterical. Man puts his machete towards Asura's face.)*

ASURA: Mosi, don't.

MOSI: Asura, I am the head girl. Please be quiet. *(Mosi turns to the Man.)* I understand your gut. I understand why you have a knife in your hand. I do. I understand that your friends are coming.

MAN: My brothers.

MOSI: I understand your bond with them. I understand that you've already done some vicious and murderous acts to get here and if you were to pause or stop right now, you might have to change your mind, and confront the fact that you are killing your neighbors.

MAN: They are cockroaches!

MOSI: They are people. Just like us. It's not too late to turn around.

MAN: I've already killed other cockroaches.

MOSI: Do you think by calling them "bugs" they stop being people?

MAN: YES! THEY ARE COCKROACHES! I am not here to argue with a child. Hand over your Tutsis! Now, or you will all die.

MOSI: No.

MAN: Do you think I am too weak to end the lives of some over-privileged girls? You have no idea what I am capable of. Or what I have even done today. The world will see what Rwanda is capable of.

MOSI: If you kill us, Rwanda, will become known as a land of blood.

MAN: It already is a land of blood. But I can't stop it. The wheel is already moving. Now the whole world will see. We will not suffer quietly any more. I can't stop the violence. It's just going to continue.

MOSI: You can stop it.

MAN: I can't. It's already started. The militia will be here very soon.

MOSI: Say no. *(Long pause and then quieter.)* Say no. *(She approaches him so slowly it aches, perhaps she touches his stomach tentatively, like a child might touch her father.)* There has to be some light inside of you still.

MAN: No. That was taken, along with my mother, father, and sister. It was taken by the cockroaches.

MOSI: It wasn't taken, you gave it up, when you picked up that machete. When you listened to hate radio or your misguided friends and decided the enemy was your neighbor. You are killing your own.

MAN: Give me the Tutsi girls. Or I will kill you all.

MOSI: No.

MAN: What?

MOSI: No. We are all Rwandans. We are all Hutus. We are all Tutsis. We are Muslims. We are Catholic. We are Belgians. We are Westerners. We are Arica. We are all sisters. And for me to say that we are not connected, that we are not the same, is weak. These are my sisters. And that is all I know.

MAN: So none of you will hand over the Tutsis?

KHATITI: No.

LAYLA: No.

SALA: No.

LULA: No.

ASURA: No.

MOSI: No.

MAN: Then you will all die with the rest of the cockroaches.

ASURA: And we will die as sisters.

MAN: Come outside. My brothers are coming. I hear them. *(Calls out the door.)* Josiah, I've got a bunch of them. The list was right. I'll be right there! Yes, brother! Those that stand together are those who fight. Those that stand together are those that fight! Outside cockroaches! Get out here before the sunsets. Stop hiding. *(Asura turns away from the window for the last time. Mosi takes Asura's hand.)*

MOSI: Asura.

ASURA: Come be brave with me, my friend. My sister. My Mosi. We're doing what is right. *(Asura and Mosi walk to the center, holding hands.)*

MAN: Up against the wall. Now. *(The twins, Lula and Layla follow behind Mosi and Asura. Lula presses her face into her sister's back as they cross.)* Cockroaches, I said now. *(Khatiti stands up slowly. She falls to her knees in a wail. The man forces her up and she runs to the others. Sala walks slowly over to the group.)*

MAN: Now. *(Sala takes Khatiti's hand. The lights dim. There is a silhouette of five girls holding hands. The man falls to his knees, he stands up weakly. There is no question what he will do. The last image is of the girls standing together, joined forever. The man's machete is raised in their direction.)*

(Blackout.)

(The End)

Brian Podnos and John Rengstorff in REUNION
in The Riant Theatre's Strawberry One-Act Festival Summer 2007
at The American Theater of Actors in NYC

REUNION

By Brian Podnos

Dedicated to my family, whose support has proven infinite; as well as John Rengstorff and Shidan Majidi, your help workshopping was invaluable.

Brian Podnos is a recent graduate of Binghamton University. He has acted professionally since the age of eight, performing in various commercials, television shows, plays and movies. Brian is a member of the Screen Actors Guild as well as the American Federation of Television and Radio Artists. New to the writing scene, *Reunion* is Brian's first production and published work, but will not be his last.

Reunion debuted in the Summer of 2007 at the American Theatre of Actors in New York City. It won the Best Play award in the Riant Theatre's Summer 2007 Strawberry One-Act Festival with the following cast:

BILL   John Rengstorff
PETER   Brian Podnos

This play was directed by Shidan Majidi.

CAST OF CHARACTERS

BILL, A man in his late fifties.
PETER, A man in his late twenties.

A WORK STUDY:
(Stage left sits a large, heavy, wooden desk. A computer laptop rests off to one side of it, a pile of filled binders on the other side. Behind the desk, a large bookshelf, the top half of which is filled with more binders. Each of these are labeled with a different clients' name. The bottom half of the bookshelf is scattered with a few novels here and

there. *Two bottles of liquor, (one full and one half-empty), a couple of glasses and a bucket of ice lay on the desk within arms reach of BILL. A chair sits in the corner of stage right.*

BILL, He wears an unbuttoned white shirt and a loose tie. A pair of big horn-rimmed glasses hangs on the edge of his nose, frequently slipping off only to be caught by the string attached to them. His thinned and remaining hair is styled into a comb over to cover the bald spot in the middle. He has not shaved in a couple of days and there is noticeable scruff. BILL is tapping a pen on an opened binder as he glances back and forth between the computer and his work. He holds the swagger of a worn down man who has spent his life working at a desk. His sunken face hangs with weariness as he pauses to drink his whiskey.

PETER enters, Thin, wearing jeans, a plain T-shirt and a khaki jacket over it. He is carrying a backpack with him. His face is clean-shaven and his features are torn between the look of a man suffering from insomnia and of one enjoying a revitalized energy. There are noticeable bags under his eyes but a youthful vigor has taken over his body. PETER enters slowly, first peeking his head in and then enters fully but cautiously as if not to disturb BILL. It is not until he is fully in the room that he is noticed. They stare at each other for a full five seconds before words are exchanged.)

PETER: Glad to see me? *(More silence, more staring.)* The door was open. *(BILL closes binder, punches a few keys in his laptop and closes it, takes off his glasses.)* Hard at work, always the worker.*(BILL pours himself a drink, leans back in his chair.)* I don't understand why I never hunkered down and worked like you. I tried, God knows I did. I'd sit up there at my desk, I'd sit and open my books and just stare. Well that's not exactly true, I'd read about three lines of whatever god-awful schoolbook I was assigned and then stare. I don't know, guess some people got it and some people don't. But I tried, that's the important part, eh? *(Silence, PETER takes out a cigarette.)* Mind if I have one of these? *(Lights it.)*

BILL: Hey what-Yes I mind please don't do that.

(PETER takes a drag.)

PETER: Oh, sorry. *(Takes another drag.)* I missed this place. It's so homey isn't it? I mean just walking in the front door and seeing those old color schemes on the wall. Mom certainly had colorful taste didn't she? What is that in the living room, is that magenta or just purple?

BILL: I guess magenta I don't really know.

PETER: Yeah, I like magenta, it sounds nicer than purple. Oh, how lovely a wall, what color is that beautiful paint? Why it's magenta of course! It's got that angelic tone in it right? I probably would have taken purple and not thought twice but mom was good at getting the color schemes of each room just perfect. I noticed you left them the same. I hope you don't mind, I took a walk around.

BILL: I uh, suppose not. Did you just, don't ash on that floor! Why would you do that? What are you stupid?

PETER: My apologies. *(Beat.)* I took a walk around the neighborhood too. I figured it would be the same. But no, it isn't! It's all different. The people are all different. The kids are all different. Not one kid at the basketball court. It's beautiful out, no basketball. Can you believe that? Probably starting their lives a little earlier or something. Going to parties and smoking cigarettes and pot and hooking up with girls and getting them pregnant and having abortions and goin' in and out of rehab. Damned kids getting older every day.

BILL: You asked on the floor again, didn't I just say not to do that?

PETER: Did I?

BILL: Just put it out.

PETER: I remember when I was a kid and it was nice out. Always playing b-ball. I'd play for hours at a time. Remember? Ha, yea, that's right. I'd play for along time. Come home when the sun came down. You know sometimes I'd wake up and just go to the courts. Bring a sandwich, some water and just go right there. It was a great life, being a kid.

BILL: Would you put it out?

PETER: I'd play so long I couldn't pick up a garbage bag. I'd play till my legs were rubber. And who cares what game I pick up, as long as I get some action. There was always action too. No action today though, no kids out at all. They're playing their video games and jerking off into socks. They got no fresh air. No iron in their souls. No action anywhere.

BILL: PUT IT OUT!

PETER: This?

BILL: Yes! That! You know that! Put it out Jesus Christ.

PETER: Where should I put it, there's no ashtrays. I don't want to be rude, but where can I put it out? In your glass? No, that would be even more discourteous. That's no way to treat a gracious host. Here, I know. *(Pulls up one arm sleeve.)* This should do the trick. *(Begins to slowly put the cigarette towards his arm.)*

BILL: What are you doing?

PETER: Putting it out. I already have a permanent bulls eye to aim for.

BILL: Stop it. Be serious for once.

PETER: Tell me I'm not serious.

BILL: *(Staring at the cigarette moving closer and closer.)* Okay, okay I believe you. Stop it please!

PETER: There's no ashtrays and I don't want to be bad-mannered.

BILL: Put it in the bucket, the bucket! The Bucket!

(PETER stops the movement of his cigarette, very close to his arm.)

PETER: The ice bucket?

BILL: Yes, yes the bucket please!

PETER: I really don't want to seem ungracious though.

BILL: Please put it there?

PETER: Alright. *(Does so.)* Mom always said an ungracious guest is an undeserving one. I always try to be mannered. Remember when we went to your boss's house and I knocked over my glass? Remember?

BILL: No.

PETER: Oh you remember. I knocked that glass right off the table. You got that look in your eyes, my god I was scared. I near pissed my pants I was so scared, knew how much I would pay for it later. I knew! Remember?

BILL: No, I don't.

PETER: Yeah maybe you don't. I guess why would you. Ha, that's right, I'm an idiot sometimes.

(Silence.)

BILL: Got a job?

PETER: I do. They found me one after I got out, at the grocery store. Really making my way to the top this time. No but, I'm doing it, working the register, earning money. Doing my part. Being a good citizen. Oh, I'm out by the way.

BILL: *(Chuckles a bit.)* I see that. Early.

PETER: I was good. Very courteous.

BILL: *(Guffaws more heartily at this.)* I bet you were. *(PETER does not respond to this and BILL cuts off his laughing.)* So how long you, uh—

PETER: A week or so.

BILL: I see. You, need money?

PETER: *(Smiles.)* No thanks.

BILL: So you want to move back in?

PETER: *(Now it's PETER'S turn to laugh, adding sardonically.)* Yeah.

BILL: Right … well, it's good to see you finally on your own. You're making your way just like the rest of us. That's a good thing. Nothing wrong with earning your way.

PETER: No sir. Mind if I have a drink?

BILL: Help yourself.

PETER: *(Truly shocked.)* Wow. I didn't think you'd laxed this much over the years. Even when I came of age you still never let me have a drink. You and mom both, hated seeing me with any type of alcohol. I always thought it was a laugh coming from you. Well, this really does mark a change. I'm going to take a drink with my father. My first drink with my Dad, I wish I had a camera.

BILL: Funny.

PETER: I'm serious! This just might be the sweetest moment of my long life. Let's do this right, let's give it a good cheer.

BILL: Wait, should you have this. Are you allowed?

PETER: I didn't go because, don't worry alright? I'm fine, besides I wouldn't pass this opportunity up for the world. My first drink with Daddio? Get outta here.

BILL: *(Wearily.)* Alright.

PETER: We need a good cheer, you know any good ones?

BILL: A couple I suppose.

PETER: I know one that's real good. I heard it a while ago, it's an old British Royal Navy's cheer unless I heard wrong. Anyways it goes like this. Ready? This is gonna be a good one, pops. I mean it. This actually makes me kinda happy. I'm earning my way and I'm drinking with you. I'm finally a man, right?

BILL: I'm happy too. It's been a while since we … it's been a while.

PETER: It certainly has. Alright how about this, you do the first cheer and I'll make the second one.

BILL: *(Takes binder off desk and places it on the shelf. Places eyeglasses on laptop and pours two glasses with a shot in each.)* To … a long silence rescinded, and finally growing up. *(BILL takes his drink, PETER hesitates a moment and then drinks. BILL fills up glasses again.)* Your turn. Pete?

PETER: Hm? Oh, yeah. This is one of my favorites. Ready for it? You're gonna have to repeat after me, it's a few lines. *(Holds up glass, BILL follows suit.)* To the wind that blows.

BILL: To the wind that blows.

PETER: And the ship that goes.

BILL: And the ship that goes.

PETER: And the lass that loves the sailor.

BILL: And the lass that loves the sailor.

PETER: To sweethearts and wives may they never meet.

BILL: *(Beat.)* To sweethearts and wives may they never meet.

(PETER drinks, BILL hesitates a moment and then drinks as well.)

PETER: I'll take one to relax with if you don't mind. *(BILL fills up a glass and hands it to him. PETER takes the chair at stage right and sits down for the first time. Sips his drink lightly.)* You always did have the good stuff. I never took anything out obviously. I liked to look though, before you came home from work. Always had a nice collection at hand. Could never hold out for your drink. High and classy's your theme.

BILL: Yeah, so how'd you get here? Did you take a cab or something?

PETER: No I walked.

BILL: From where?

PETER: I live on the West Side now.

BILL: You walked all the way from the West side?

PETER: It's a beautiful day.

BILL: That must be fifteen miles away.

PETER: I like walking. It's nice.

BILL: You could have just called me.

PETER: I like it because it's solitary. It's peaceful, there's no one to bother me. Just me, my cigarettes and my thoughts. And of course the wonder of a sun filled day. Grass is always greener, people are always happier.

BILL: Why here?

PETER: Sorry?

BILL: I mean I'm happy you're here, I'm just surprised you're here. Why'd you come?

(Beat.)

PETER: I passed through the park. I sat down on a bench and just watched, you know, the world. Not one child playing, not one. Incredible. A few old couples walking around, a few dog walkers, but not one kid. Isn't that the damnedest thing? Kids wanting to stay home. I don't understand it. *(Beat.)* I was listening to this one old couple arguing with each other. I walked behind them, they never noticed. Amazing that people their age can still yell like that. It brought a smile to my face. They were yelling about whether he knew someone or not. She kept screaming at him. It was so funny Dad, she kept screaming and wouldn't let him get a word out. Every time he tried to talk it was like she already knew what was gonna come out of his mouth. It was hilarious. Then he began to hit her. He really wailed on her, he beat her good. He beat her rapid fire, it was like blamblamblamblam! It was hilarious. A regular Ali the way he was throwing them punches, and you know something? She kept yelling. Now THAT was incredible stuff. Really amazing. It didn't faze her in the least bit. Now how a 90 year old has the energy to hit anything, let alone his wife I'll never know. But she took it in stride. Knew it was coming, had to know it was coming. I mean she kept on yammering about how much of an idiot he was to think he knew so and so. Then this old bastard gave her a closed fist right on the side of her head. That shut her up finally. He, well you should'a seen his face. He was very upset I guess. It's true though. Understood. Necessary even, right? When your wife gets out of line you have to put her in her place! Eventually that doesn't even work though, and then what? You're stuck with a beaten wife that don't learn. What do you do then, right? This old bastard is fucked. He's got no power anymore. That was the funniest part too, the look of sheer desperation on his face with every hit. Despair. Desolation. He was a beaten man. Ha! A beaten man. Seriously though, it was a great event to see. Something so arbitrary and meaningless brought so much emotion out of them. I don't know, it's different now. Maybe the world's changing for this new generation of kids. I guess that makes my generation the middleman between the new and the old. The misfit of two worlds, eh?

BILL: You just, just stood there and watched all this?

PETER: What else was I going to do? Stop them?

BILL: I don't, well yes. Why didn't you stop them?

PETER: And then what? The moment I'm gone he'll be hitting her worse than before.

BILL: You don't know that.

PETER: *(Sarcastically laughing.)* Oh give me a break.

BILL: Now you listen here-

PETER: Okay, okay, I don't want to argue.

BILL: No, you listen-

PETER: Dad?

BILL: Would you stop interrupting me for god's sake? Now, you don't know anything about the relationship between a man and a woman. Sometimes—

PETER: Sometimes it's necessary to go a long distance out of the way in order to come back a short distance correctly.

BILL: What the hell does that mean?

PETER: It's Edward Albee.

BILL: That one of your writers?

PETER: *(Beat.)* Yes. He's one of my-

BILL: Don't bring any of that BS into my home. You know I hate that—

PETER: Dad?

BILL: Just don't bring it here.

PETER: DAD!! Would you fucking listen to me for a second!?

BILL: *(Finally understanding that Peter has something to say.)* What?

PETER: I want to reconcile.

BILL: Reconcile.

PETER: Is it that hard to believe? *(Beat.)* Mom would want this wouldn't she?

BILL: I suppose she would.

PETER: Of course she would! Has she been dead so long that you don't even know what she would have wanted? It's only been five years.

BILL: Can we just stop talking about—

PETER: To the day.

BILL: Oh. I see. *(Silence, they stare at each other.)* Well, what the hell are you staring at?

PETER: *(Breaking the stare.)* Nothing.

BILL: Yeah.

PETER: Those all your clients?

BILL: Yes.

PETER: You've been working on those a long time.

BILL: Too long.

PETER: Too long?

BILL: Way too long.

PETER: Quit.

BILL: Excuse me?

PETER: You heard me, quit.

BILL: *(Laughs at this.)* That's a great idea.

PETER: No, I'm serious. You said it yourself, you've been working too long. So stop. Why is that so ridiculous?

BILL: What am I going to do if I quit my job?

PETER: I don't know, anything you want?

BILL: *(Pugnaciously.)* Anything? Anything. God, you still don't get it. You live in this fantasy world. Quit my job. You don't just change careers on a damned whim Pete. The world doesn't work that way. You've been at this grocery job, what? A couple weeks? Come back and talk to me in a couple decades. You're finally learning to become a man, finally, and that's a good thing, if you keep it up. I know the statistics, chances are you're gonna end up right back where you were a couple years ago. Don't think I'm not supportive, I am. But that doesn't mean I'm not doubtful of your dedication. I don't want to see you coming here begging for money. I'm not going to give it to you. You're on your own from here on out.

PETER: *(Furiously, but after regaining a friendly composure instantly.)* I've never asked you for money. Never.

BILL: No, I guess not. Don't think you can start though. Look, I'm not saying this to be mean, I'm just saying the god honest truth. I believe in you though. Don't get me wrong. I believe that you'll finally make a man of yourself. I believe that you'll put away your stupid fantasies of success and earn a living the way it has to be done, with work.

PETER: Yes sir.

BILL: I raised you right. No one can tell me I didn't raise you good. I've seen you play your sports, I read your stories, I've been good to you. I put food on the dinner table, didn't I? I did the work. I did it for you and your mother. And I never ran out on you. A lot of people, well I didn't. I took responsibility. And all I asked for was a nice home to come to. A respectful family. That was all I wanted from either of you. Just respect for what I had to do. You know my father used to beat me every other day if he was in the mood. He'd switch my back up till it bled, all the time! Every other day! It was rough yes, but I learned—

(The following dialogue between Peter and Bill should overlap each other.)

PETER: *(Crying like a baby.)* WAAAAAAHHHHHHHHH!

BILL: What, what, what—

PETER: WAAAAAAAAHHHHHHH! WAAAAAAHHHHHHHH!

BILL: What are you doing? Stop. Stop that.

PETER: Oh come on, don't play dumb. That sound is indistinguishable.

BILL: I, what?

PETER: The sound, I know it was years ago but I've got the sound right.

BILL: No, I—

PETER: WAAAAAAHHHHHHHHH!

BILL: Why are you yelling that! I don't understand what you're doing!

PETER: WAAAHHHHH!

BILL: SHUT UP! STOP IT!

(Bill raises his hand ready to strike, but stops suddenly and backs away. Peter pulls out a black kit from his back pack and goes to the desk.)

BILL: *(Quietly at first.)* Is that? Is, is that?

PETER: It is.

BILL: You son of a bitch. *(PETER ignores him as he unzips the kit and opens it.)* Once a junkie always a junkie. *(PETER takes out an arm strap, begins to tie a knot around his arm.)* What do you, what the hell are you doing? I always knew it. You're no, no son of mine. Get out! Out of my house! *(PETER ignores.)* Little bastard, I'll be damned if you, you're not too old yet you son of a bitch.

(BILL takes off belt and moves towards PETER. PETER takes the black kit, picks it up and slams it down hard on the table while letting out a loud yell. BILL stops his movement.)

PETER: Am I looking now?

BILL: Junkie bastard.

PETER: What are you going to do? What!? *(BILL stumbles back a bit, stares at PETER. PETER sits back down, opens the kit and ties a knot around his arm.)* It's only a couple grams, calm down.

(This next action takes place as BILL and PETER speak, PETER takes out a pre-filled syringe.)

BILL: The balls, the balls. In my home.

PETER: You know what the great thing is about china white, smack, Judas, tecata, the black pearl? The great thing is the lucidity of the experience. Everything makes sense. Nothing gets in the way of total clarity.

BILL: You want to kill yourself, you do it away from me. You hear that? Away from me! I don't know you. I don't want to know you, I want you gone. I want rest from all this. I want rest. Please just, just leave me alone.

PETER: You'll never see me again after today.

BILL: Okay. *(Starts to exit towards stage right.)*

PETER: Where do you think you're going?

BILL: I need fresh air.

PETER: No, I don't think so.

BILL: Don't you dare tell me what to do in my home. *(PETER stands up and stares at him. BILL tries to leave but PETER shoves him into the desk.)* What the hell are you doing?

PETER: I don't want to hurt you, but I need to talk.

BILL: We're done here.

PETER: I don't want to hurt you but I will. All I want to do is talk to you, and then you'll never see me again. Just a conversation, alright?

(BILL takes a few moments and then sits down in his chair.)

BILL: Talk if you're going to for god's sake.

(Beat.)

PETER: You know the moments that stick closest to you? The first moments, first experiences. With everything, you know?

BILL: Oh god.

PETER: First time I kissed a girl. First time I smoked a cigarette. First time I woke up in a strange place. First time I begged for a fix. First time I sat at the bottom of the stairs and listened. First time Mom put me in a tub of ice. All those memories stick.

BILL: I can't do this.

PETER: The first time was so good. I mean it was fucking incredible, Dad. I just sank into my couch. Felt like I went inside it, wrapped up in a blanket of nirvana. You look at life, at all this shit and only one thought runs through your head. Who gives a fuck? Sometimes, when you get a real good fix, you nod in and out. That's the best. I've heard it called the sleep of angels. Sleep of angels, it's so true.

BILL: *(Practically bursting into tears.)* Stop it, stop, stop blaming. This isn't my fault! It's not my fault you turned out this way. I tried. I always try. I do what's needed to survive damnit! My life is a bed of roses, yeah, I got no troubles, sure. You see me turning to that junk? No! Yeah, I tend to have a drink here and there, but I never once thought of going to that. I just, I, I ... ugh, god! When my father ran out on us, who do you think got put to work. Me! I was the oldest, I had to take care of the family. I wasn't even out of high school. Me! Peddling around town in that cart, that stupid cart, like a damned fool. All day long I worked, all the way into the night. Every day. Every god-forsaken day was the same thing. Out before the sun's awake and back when the sun's gone to bed. For scraps, for nothing, for survival! I did it for them and for you guys, you and your mother. I did it for everyone. I don't do anything for myself. Don't you get that I tried to give you a life that was better than mine! Better! And now this happens and for what? You had a good life. She had a good life. What happened to my life? What about me? When I found her, like that. I don't get it. I just don't get anything anymore.

   (Pours himself a big glass.)
   PETER: I killed a dog.
   BILL: What?
   PETER: A dog, big one too. I think I killed it. Real nice thing. Always licking my hand when I said hello. I took a baseball bat and beat it. I killed the dog.
   BILL: Why would you do that?
   PETER: Its eyes filled with blood. Took longer then I thought it would. Once I started I couldn't stop though. I killed a dog, then I went home and read a book. I read a lot. *(Beat.)* I just want to do something meaningful. *(Beat.)* I do love you. *(Beat.)* I don't know why. *(Beat.)* I hate … I hate. *(Beat.)* But I also love. That's why I did it. I loved the dog. I loved her so much. So god damned much. I just couldn't stand by and watch him suffer any more. So I killed him. *(Beat.)* Do you get it?
   BILL: No, I don't. I don't understand you.
   PETER: *(Reciting lines from the poem, A Dream Within a Dream, by Edgar Allen Poe.)* I stand amid the roar Of a surf-tormented shore, And I hold within my hand Grains of the golden sand—How few! Yet how they creep Through my fingers to the deep, While I weep—while I weep! *(Beat.)* Do you get it? Do you understand me now?
   BILL: Pete I'm not good, I don't hear that stuff well.
   PETER: *(Recites A Poison Tree, by William Blake.)* I was angry with my friend: I told my wrath, my wrath did end. I was angry with my foe; I told it not, my wrath did grow. *(Beat.)* Do you get it?
   BILL: Why, I don't, what are you—
   PETER: *(Recites lines from O Captain! My Captain!, by Walt Whitman.)* My Captain does not answer, his lips are pale and still; My father does not feel my arm, he has no pulse nor will. *(Beat.)* Do you get me? Do you? Dad? Daddy?
   BILL: No! Stop it! Right now! Get out of here! Get the hell out!
   PETER: You know I told them what they wanted to hear, at the clinic. I went through the system, I had to, to get to this moment. Remember this moment.

This is a first. I could have ended it at any time. I was really ready to, came so close a couple times. I mean very close. I almost just gave up. *(Beat.)* I had a vision, Dad. I could see myself right here at this moment. See? I saw this all like it was a memory. I know what's going to happen and it's fucking beautiful. It's the only way. It's meaningful. *(Beat.)* Sunday mornings. Pancakes. Remember that smell? I'll never forget waking up to it. That smell, it invaded my dreams. That smell was for me, shining like a smiling sun. *(Beat.)* She was beautiful wasn't she?

BILL: She's dead! She's fucking dead! Gone!

PETER: Why didn't she leave a note? At least one for me? Maybe you found it and just ripped it up. Maybe she left something that explained everything and you threw it out. I guess it doesn't matter anymore. I guess she never really had to explain. Recognition though, where was my recognition? My goodbye. *(Beat.)* Did you find her after, or maybe you were there the whole time. Did she say goodbye to you? Did she look you in the eye? Were you watching when she did it? Or was it you that did it? Did you do it? Was it you? Huh? Daddddddyyyyyyyy, was it you?

BILL: *(Rushes over to PETER, throws him to the ground and begins punching him in the face.)* How dare you! You no good son of a bitch! How dare you speak to me like that! I loved her! I loved her! I didn't do anything to her! I didn't do anything!

PETER: *(These next screams become muffled as the punching continues and then fade away into silence.)* I'm looking! Daddy I'm looking! I'm looking I am I'm looking I'm looking I'm looking I'm looking!

BILL: *(Still punching.)* Shut up! Shut up will you! Damn you to hell! Why don't you ever shut up! Why why why! *(As if shocked out of a nightmare, stumbles back.)* My god … I … oh Jesus. *(PETER lays still.)* What did I do? *(Beat.)* Peter? Pete? Petey? Baby?

(Lights slowly fade to black as BILL stares at PETER from a distance.)

(The End)

*Tashion Folkes as NIKKI and Miebaka Yohannes as SHAREEM
in FIGHTING FIRES in
The Riant Theatre's Strawberry One-Act Festival Summer 2007
at The American Theater of Actors in NYC*

FIGHTING FIRES

By Von H. Washington, Sr.

Von H. Washington, Ph.D., has written, directed, performed in and/or super-vised more than 300 theatrical productions. He is a member of SAG, AFTRA, and AEA. He has worked as an actor, playwright, teacher, director, and theatrical consultant. Among his present activities is directing WPI, a theatrical, educational Company, created by Von and his wife Fran. He has written more than 25 plays. Among them are *Remnants from Senegal, Conspiracy, Dancing with Yesterday* and *The Black American Dream.* His play *Seven Stops to Freedom*, winner of the 2000 Junteenth New Works competition at the University of Louisville, was recently produced in China and South Africa. This past year, *Rosa Parks: More Than a Bus Story,* was sponsored by the National Black Theatre Touring Circuit, of New York City and *Fighting Fires* was the winner of the 2006 playwright's competition at the Black Arts and Cultural Center of Kalamazoo, MI.

Fighting Fires made its New York City debut as a finalist in the Riant Theatre's Summer 2007 Strawberry One Act Festival at the Leonard Nimoy Thalia Theatre at Symphony Space, 2537 Broadway at 95th Street with the following cast, in order of appearance:

SHAREEM	Miebaka Yohannes
NIKKI	Tashion Folkes
SYLVIA	Crystal Lilly
FRANK	Ralph McCain

The play was directed by Kim Weston-Moran

CAST OF CHARACTERS

SHAREEM, a young black male
NIKKI, Shareem's lady love

27

SYLVIA, Shareem's mother
FRANK, Shareem's father

SCENE 1
(Each actor performs as character and storyteller. They talk and interact with each other and the audience as the dialogue suggests. They also move in and out of the scenes when necessary. All are on stage for the entire play. At curtain, SHAREEM stands with his mother and father at center stage as if in a family portrait. NIKKI stands slightly off to the right. After a moment, the portrait breaks up and SHAREEM sits center stage, reading a book. The others sit close by, but in separate areas where they perform minimal tasks suggesting that they are preparing for the action to come.)

NIKKI: I first I saw Shareem during my sophomore year in high school. I remember it like it was yesterday because it was an unusually cold day and I had to walk home from work, because I had missed the last bus. When I got close to home, two neighborhood thugs, REGGIE and KIP, old enough to be my daddy, started wolfin' at me. "Hey baby, I sure would like to get my"—well, you get the picture. Then Shareem appeared. He seemed to come out of nowhere like he was batman or something, and with a few well chosen words, he made 'em stop.

SHAREEM: *(As if speaking to KIP and REGGIE.)* Hey, come on brothas! Leave the Sistah alone! She ain't who you lookin' for.

NIKKI: I thought that was special, a perfect stranger reaching out to help a lady in distress. And he was right. They didn't want to have nothing to do with me. *(Pats her purse.)* I saw him two more times in that very same spot and both times he waved. Then, the very next time, he crossed over to where I was walking and laid his little rap on me.

SHAREEM: Hey. How you doing? Everything okay?

NIKKI: Yeah, I'm okay. At first he was acting like he was my big brother or something, but that didn't last too long. From the beginning, he appeared strong and self-assured. He was also charming, sensitive ... and sexy. I found out that we went to the same school ... and he was a good student. Not like a lot of other boys I knew.

SHAREEM: Nikki was a real sweet girl. And, she wasn't no push over, either. Her family was living in a tough part of the city and she was going to school and holding down a job at the same time. She was okay with me.

NIKKI: My daddy got me a gun. *(Pats her purse again.)* He told me it was to protect me from men like Reggie and Kip. That's why I wasn't too worried about them.

SHAREEM: She told me all about her gun but I already knew that Reggie and Kip weren't going to bother her, they were my watching buddies. But, I didn't tell her about that, and anyway, it gave me a front to run my piece.

NIKKI: And it was a good piece to run. But wasn't no first night thing tho. And Even though we didn't start dating until late in our junior year, I thought—you know—he was that special person God made just for me. He seemed to have it all together. He would always tell me that he was waiting for the right moment to do what he had to do and then things would be all right.

SHAREEM: Nikki, as soon as I fill in a few blanks, everything's gonna be all right.

NIKKI: I didn't know what he meant then … I thought he was talking about us.

SYLVIA: It wasn't always easy to know what Shareem was thinking or talking about. I gave birth to the boy, took care of him all those years, and I still didn't know him … couldn't understand that street lingo. That hip hop jive … and, it was about that time that he started that stuff about blanks.

SHAREEM: Mama, if you don't fill in the blanks, you go around with a lot of empty spaces where there should be stuff. That's what's wrong with brothas and sistahs now. Dealing with too many blanks.

SYLVIA: Blanks? What kind of blanks?

SHAREEM: The big blanks, Mama, the big blanks.

SYLVIA: Now what did that mean? I thought it was from some of that music he was listening to. Sometimes, he was down right confusing. He was an outgoing boy but … private … but still fun to be around. And at times he's very talkative. I should say, talkative about the things he wanted to talk about. Other things were sort of taboo, like his father.

SHAREEM: I ain't got nothing to say about him! He ain't here is he?

SYLVIA: That was about it for that subject—short and not so sweet. I never knew how Shareem really felt about his father. Or how his father felt about him, for that matter. That's why when it happened it was such a surprise to me.

FRANK: *(Slightly on the defense.)* I cared about my son … but … things weren't always the way I wanted them to be. Life's not a straight line you know? Like the poet says, "there's tacks and splinters and boards torn up?"

SYLVIA: Langston Hughes. That's who wrote that poem and he really liked to say, "Life for me ain't been no crystal stair." Well … he was right about that.

SHAREEM: *(As if talking to his father.)* But, if you got blanks in your life, you go around with a lot of emptiness. There comes a time when you have to fill in the blanks.

NIKKI: Shareem and I spent some quality time together during our senior year. We were doing college prep together and we used that as an excuse to get together as much as we could. We always met at his place when his mother was at work. I don't know if he knew it, but the day of the big fire, I was planning on getting something straight, too. *(She joins him at center stage.)*

SHAREEM: *(After a long kiss and or embrace.)* You better watch yourself girl. You gonna start a fire you can't put out.

NIKKI: What if I don't want to put it out?

SHAREEM: Well … right now you gonna have to put it out because I don't have the right equipment.

NIKKI: Shareem, nooooo. I thought you said—

SHAREEM: I know what I said but I just don't have them with me right now. I left them at home. We can take care of business later.

NIKKI: What makes you think the fire's gonna be burning later?

SHAREEM: If it goes out that quick, it's not a very good fire.

NIKKI: You're awfully sure of your self, aren't you?

SHAREEM: No I'm not. I just know what a good fire feels like and you make good fires.

NIKKI: Well, if they so good, why don't you remember to bring things to fight them with?

SHAREEM: Because I knew if I got too involved with putting out a fire, I wouldn't do what I need to do, and time is running out.

NIKKI: Time for what? *(Returning to audience.)* If I had any sense, I would have known that something was up because almost nothing could stop Shareem when he started tending to a good fire. And he was right. It was a good fire. But, I did know a little something was up because right after I left his place that day, I saw him talking to Reggie and Kip. I had never seen him talk to them before.

SYLVIA: I should have known something was bothering him. A mother is supposed to know these things. I mean, I knew he had little problems, here and there. I just didn't know what was smoldering underneath, until I was standing right in the middle of it.

SHAREEM: Hey Mama, did you know that most black families are like ours?

SYLVIA: What's that—broke?

(They both laugh.)

SHAREEM: Well … that too. But in most of them there is just one parent. Especially now-a-days.

SYLVIA: Most of them? Is that true? Who told you that?

SHAREEM: *(Motions to the book he is reading.)* Read it in this book. Some people say it goes back to slavery and the slave masters. Who do you think is responsible, now?

SYLVIA: *(To audience.)* I didn't answer that question. I think he wanted me to say black men ... because that's who I always blamed. But that day, I didn't answer. I had tried to stop doing that.

SHAREEM: I mean, who's ultimately responsible for keeping a family together?

SYLVIA: He hadn't seen his father for years. And to be truthful, I didn't ... well, let's just leave it at that. He was so young when Frank and I went our separate ways. So I was surprised when he up and told me about seeing him.

SHAREEM: I'm going to see my dad.

SYLVIA: *(To SHAREEM.)* Your dad? What dad?

SHAREEM: My dad ... Frank. Remember?

SYLVIA: *(Pause)* You going to see Frank? When did this come about?

SHAREEM: The other day.

SYLVIA: Now wait a minute Shareem. If I'm right, you don't even know what your dad looks like. You've only seen him—

SHAREEM: *(Irritated)* You don't have to remind me, I know!

SYLVIA: *(Carefully)* Well then how are you gonna see him if you don't know—

SHAREEM: Mama, there are certain things I know that you don't know I know. Okay?

SYLVIA: Oh I see. *(Playfully)* So you think you grown now and you don't have to tell anybody what's goin on?

SHAREEM: *(Bitterness creeping in.)* I been grown for a long time, Mama. Haven't you noticed? Your little man is a big man now.

SYLVIA: *(To the audience.)* I knew I was in trouble then. I could hear it in his voice. I had been calling him my little man for so many years. And yeah, I told him—I don't know how many times—that he had to be the man of the house because his daddy ... well, you get the picture. *(To SHAREEM.)* How you gonna see him, Shareem? You don't know where he lives.

SHAREEM: Yes I do.

SYLVIA: Since when?

SHAREEM: Since a long time ago.

SYLVIA: How long ago, Shareem?

SHAREEM: Since we moved from 47th street.

SYLVIA: What! Forty Seventh street? But ... You were just—

SHAREEM: Yeah, I know.

SYLVIA: I didn't think you would remember that.

SHAREEM: Yep, I remembered.

SYLVIA: Why didn't you tell me?

SHAREEM: For what?

SYLVIA: *(Irritated)* So I could say something, know something. I mean, we are family.

SHAREEM: By whose definition?

SYLVIA: Don't pull that school shit on me boy! Now tell me what's going on!

SHAREEM: *(Self assured)* Nothing Mama. I'm just gonna see my dad.

SYLVIA: About what?

SHAREEM: He said he wanted to see me about a few things. Men stuff. You know. He's gonna fill in a few blanks.

SYLVIA: Now don't start that street stuff again. Tell me what's going on. *(Pause)* Do you want me to go with you?

SHAREEM: For what?

SYLVIA: I don't know for what, Shareem. I haven't thought about this like you have. *(Pause)* You know he's married and has another family now.

SHAREEM: Mama, don't keep calling us a family! We were never a family. *(Angrily closes the book he was reading and throws it near SYLVIA'S feet.)*

SYLVIA: *(After picking up book.)* Books. What good are they? They always start things they can't finish.

FRANK: *(To audience.)* It was really strange the way it happened. And, yes, I should have been suspicious. All of a sudden these two guys from the neighborhood come looking for me. I hadn't been back there in years. Not since me and Sylvia broke up.

SYLVIA: Broke up? We were never together!

FRANK: I don't think she saw it that way, but, I did. I mean, I was willing to try and make a go of it, but at the time I just didn't want … didn't want … well—

SYLVIA: *(To audience.)* He didn't want to get married. Tradition.

FRANK: Because we weren't about that.

SYLVIA: His famous saying …

FRANK: We were just building a little fire.

SYLVIA: … and it got out of hand.

NIKKI: I always wondered where Shareem got that building fires thing from.

SYLVIA: He got it from his daddy. But, Shareem didn't know that. When he was very young, I use to tell him that he was conceived in a really hot fire that got out of hand.

SHAREEM: One night I overheard her tell some of her friends that, right after I was born, she was waiting for the fireman to come and take care of the job but he said "sorry lady, I don't go into burning houses." They all had a great big laugh about that.

FRANK: I mean, if we had met under different circumstances, it could have been different. But at the time, we were just kids out there having fun. What did we call it, ah—

SYLVIA: Heatin' it up.

FRANK: Yeah, something like that.

SHAREEM: Even though I didn't see my dad, I never forgot about him. I don't think children forget about the people who give them birth. That's why I felt close to the children of slaves. They never had a choice. You know your parents are alive but you never know where they are or how they feel about you.

SYLVIA: I thought about Frank. Sometimes I wished that I would see him, just to find out how he was doing. But I knew he would never come back to the neighborhood. He never wanted to be there in the first place. And I admit, I never tried to find him.

FRANK: It was a dead end place and everybody knew it. It wasn't fit for anybody to live there, especially if you had a family.

SYLVIA: His mama lived there but he didn't get along with her. I would see her from time to time, but she didn't care about me or Shareem. I guess she had enough trouble tending to her own. She was a single mother too.

SHAREEM: I always thought he cared about me and that he knew he owed me something. I kept thinking any-day-now, he was going to come by to claim his own and ... set everything straight. After all, there were no slave masters barring the door.

FRANK: I thought about him a lot, but my hands were tied. I had a family to take care of and Shareem's mother, well ... she made it clear that she didn't care to have me coming around any more. Said it reminded her of what she wanted to forget.

SHAREEM: Kip kept telling me, *(He mimics KIP.)* "You living in a fairy tale young blood. Hit and run drivers never return to the scene of the crime ... unless you force 'em to."

NIKKI: One night Shareem and I were studying for a big test on American history and, out of the blue, he asked me—

SHAREEM: What you think about broken homes?

NIKKI: He seemed a little bit nervous when he asked me. I guess he knew that I would know he was talking about his family. I don't remember exactly what I said, but I know I didn't feel like that was right. And I did say that we needed to do something to stop that kind of stuff. But that was easy for me to say, I lived with my parents.

FRANK: Anyway, these guys from the old neighborhood came to see me. I don't know how they found me. One of them said by accident. Any way, they tell me that my son—Shareem—was in some kind of trouble and he asked them to come and get me.

SHAREEM: Reggie and Kip were the neighborhood watch dogs. They knew everything that went down. They knew where all the ex-daddies were. They had been looking for theirs since they were kids and sometimes I hung out with them to look for mine.

FRANK: They told me it was a matter of life and death. So thinking that it was my son—Shareem—I went with them. At the time I felt a little foolish because I didn't even know what Shareem looked like.

SYLVIA: Frank hadn't seen that boy in years. Half the time I didn't recognize him myself, he was growing so fast.

FRANK: I hadn't heard his name spoken out loud for a long time. But, they seemed to know so much about me, that I thought it must have been on the up-and-up.

SHAREEM: Reggie said, "we'll kidnap the Negro if we have to. It's time for him to come back to the scene of the crime and pay up."

NIKKI: Shareem and I had gotten really serious about each other and he was talking about getting married. And I liked that. So I was happy when he said—

SHAREEM: I think we should spend a whole night together, so we can know how it feels when we get married. Maybe I can fight that fire.

NIKKI: *(Excited)* I could not wait! So we told a few stupid lies, and he rented this motel room way on the other side of town. He told me to meet him there around seven o'clock and not to worry because he was setting up everything. Naturally, I went shopping. *(Mimes wearing a negligee.)*

SYLVIA: Shareem told me where he and his dad were going to meet and he said that Frank had asked for me to be there. Now that really shocked me, because the last time I saw Frank I told him, point blank—*(To FRANK.)* I never want to see you again. And … you can forget about seeing your son! *(To audience.)* And I kept my word.

FRANK: It's not like I just up and left. I tried several times to see Shareem. But Sylvia was really upset with me because I didn't—

SYLVIA: Want to get married! That's when I first moved to 47th Street. And then I moved again, so he couldn't find us. I knew he would never come looking for me. He hated that place … and I guess I was just angry.

FRANK: So I moved away for good, promising myself that I would never go back. And I kept my word.

SHAREEM: I thought about it for a long time and it was the only thing that made sense. Since neither one of my parents had tried to get us together, I felt that I had to do it myself. Anyway, the books say that a family is supposed to come together to work out their differences.

NIKKI: *(Sexually suggestive)* There's this one book that says a family that plays together stays together. Or something like that.

SHAREEM: And since my mama kept referring to us as family, I decided to make sure everybody was present when we started playing together. I include Nikki because she was gonna be my family.

NIKKI: When I got to the motel room, Shareem had everything all laid out. Candles and incense burning, and he was dressed real nice. I thought because he wanted to make a good impression on me. It was a good thing I had gone shopping. It was just like in the movies.

SHAREEM: I went over all of my plans very carefully. I didn't want to miss anything.

NIKKI: *(To SHAREEM.)* Honey, this is so nice. *(Whispering in his ear.)* Just wait one minute because I got something to show you. Don't go anywhere; I'll be right back. I got a surprise for you. *(Takes a few items from her purse. Leaves the purse but grabs her shopping bag and moves away. SHAREEM gets the purse, finds the gun, checks chamber, and puts gun in pocket.)*

SYLVIA: I took the bus to a stop close to where I was to meet Frank and Shareem. Now I might be a little dense at times but it made no sense for Frank and Shareem to be meeting in this god-forsaken-place.

SHAREEM: *(Placing books.)* I laid out all the things that I would need to help me make my point. That way, I could be quick and thorough. *(Picks up a copy of Ellison's The Invisible Man.)*

SYLVIA: It was almost out of town. Didn't make no sense at all. It was like he didn't want anybody to see him. I thought, just like Frank, always worried about what people gonna think.

FRANK: Just about the moment I was getting ready to ask these guys where we were headed, they stopped the car and told me to get out and turn around. *(Acting out the scene.)* That's when I really knew I was in trouble because both of them were acting like they were packin' heat. They said it was for my own protection and they blindfolded me.

SHAREEM: *(Calling out.)* Nikki. Don't dress up baby. I got something to show you first.

FRANK: When the blindfold was in place they grabbed my arms and tied my hands behind my back. *(Places his hands behind his back.)* All the time I was thinking, how stupid I had been. These guys might be thinking about killing me. When they gagged me, I knew I was finished. *(Turns back to the audience and places gag around his mouth, he then begins to struggle.)*

SHAREEM: Ain't that something. After all these years, I'm gonna be face to face with my daddy … the invisible man.

(SHAREEM grabs FRANK as he struggles and tries to speak. SHAREEM places him in a chair in the middle of the stage.)

NIKKI: My goodness! What's going on out there? What's that noise, Shareem?

SYLVIA: It seemed like I walked for two miles to get to that raggedy motel. But nothing prepared me for what I saw when Shareem let me into that room. *(After seeing FRANK.)* What the hell!

NIKKI: *(Enters)* My goodness. Shareem, what's going on? Who is that?

SHAREEM: It's my father.

NIKKI: Your father? How'd he get here?

(FRANK tries to move.)

SHAREEM: Sit still man. Don't make me hurt you.

SYLVIA: Shareem, what is going on? I thought you said—

SHAREEM: I know what I said. I just didn't want to take any chances.

NIKKI: What kind of chances?

SHAREEM: Ask my mother. She knows what I mean.

(FRANK attempts to talk but he is still gagged.)

SYLVIA: How am I supposed to know what you mean? You didn't tell me nothing about this.

SHAREEM: You said he never wanted to see me. So, I took a few precautions.

SYLVIA: Precautions for what?

NIKKI: Why is he all tied up and got that cloth in his mouth? That's not right.

SHAREEM: It's not supposed to be right, Nikki. Right now you don't understand. It's not what you think.

NIKKI: Well, will you please tell me what's going on so I'll know what to think?

SYLVIA: Please! Because this is like something from a horror movie. What's going on, Shareem?

(FRANK tries to speak.)

SYLVIA: And please take that thing from around his mouth.

(SYLVIA moves to untie him but SHAREEM stops her.)

SHAREEM: Please mother, don't do that.

NIKKI: But why not Shareem? What's going on?

SHAREEM: Okay, everybody just calm down. I'll explain everything.

SYLVIA: Good and make it fast because my mind is telling me to get the hell out of here. Boy what is wrong with you? I thought you said Frank wanted to see you.

(FRANK tries to speak.)

SHAREEM: He did. He just didn't know it.

SYLVIA: Now what is that supposed to mean?

NIKKI: *(Emotional)* Yeah, Shareem, what's that supposed to mean?

SYLVIA: Don't worry uh … uh, what's your name again?

NIKKI: Nikki. Nikki Glovers.

SYLVIA: Yeah, that's right. Nikki. We gonna get to the bottom of this.

(FRANK tries to speak. SHAREEM watches him intently.)

SYLVIA: Now Shareem, please take that thing from around his mouth so he can talk.

NIKKI: Yeah, Shareem. And, I would feel better if you took the blindfold off, too. And, how come you got him tied up like that?

SHAREEM: I told you, I'm gonna explain it as soon as I take care of a little business.

SYLVIA: What business? What is going on here, Shareem?

SHAREEM: *(Pause)* I brought him here to get some blanks filled in! Okay?

SYLVIA: But you said he asked to see—

SHAREEM: *(Irritated)* No, Mama! He did not ask to see me. I asked Reggie and Kip to bring him here. I needed to get some questions answered and I wasn't in a mood to hear no, so I felt I had to do this.

(FRANK tries very hard to be heard.)

SYLVIA: *(Pause)* But Shareem, there are other ways to get somebody's attention! And, there are things you don't understand, baby.

SHAREEM: Mama, I am not a baby! I'm trying to figure things out for myself—before it's too late.

SYLVIA: To late for what?

SHAREEM: For me!

SYLVIA: *(Not understanding.)* For you? For what?

SHAREEM: *(Meaning NIKKI.)* What you think she's doing here?

SYLVIA: Nikki? Well, I thought she was your girlfriend—

SHAREEM: I'm talking about now … in this room with us now?

SYLVIA: Well, I don't know. I guess she's …

SHAREEM: She's here because she's got to know too mom. She's got a stake in this too.

SYLVIA: Know what, Shareem?

SHAREEM: Know what kind of man I am.

NIKKI: But I already know that.

SHAREEM: No you don't. You only know a part of me. You don't know what's hidden underneath … and neither do I. He's the only one who knows. And since he didn't stay around to share it with me, I'm gonna get it now.

NIKKI: How you gonna get it if you don't let him talk?

SHAREEM: I'm gonna let him talk … as soon as I'm ready.

NIKKI: He sounds like he needs to talk now, Shareem.

SYLVIA: Shareem, why do you have him tied up? There's no reason for you to tie him up. I don't think he'll run away.

SHAREEM: Why not? He ran away before?

SYLVIA: Well—

(FRANK shakes his head and tries very hard to be understood.)

NIKKI: Shareem, what are you planning on doing?

SHAREEM: I'm gonna ask him some questions and if I don't like the answers, I'm gonna do to him what he did to me.

SYLVIA: What is that?

NIKKI: Yeah, Shareem, what are you talking about?

SHAREEM: You'll see … just give me a few minutes.

NIKKI: But, Shareem, you're not going to hurt him are you?

SHAREEM: He hurt me!

NIKKI: Yeah, but Shareem, that was different.

SYLVIA: Yes, son, what you are talking about is different.

SHAREEM: How is it different, Mama? Pain is pain. I feel pain because of him because of what he did. And I think he's supposed to pay for that.

NIKKI: Pay for it how, Shareem? How you gonna make him pay?

SHAREEM: You'll see … you'll see. Just give me a moment!

SYLVIA: *(Backing off.)* Okay, son, go ahead. We'll wait.

(SHAREEM takes off FRANKS blindfold. For a moment, they sit and look at each other.)

SHAREEM: First of all, I want to make it clear to you that I am sorry I had to do this, this way. But when I thought about everything, I got angry, because you hadn't come on your own to—

SYLVIA: Let him talk now son, please.

SHAREEM: *(Ignores her.)* And I know that what I'm planning to do could get me into trouble; or it could make me feel better. It may not make everybody happy with me but everybody ain't been happy with me anyway. Especially you.

SYLVIA: Shareem please, this is not right.

SHAREEM: *(Pause)* I also think you should know that I have had you on my mind for a long time. You've been like a fire, burning inside of me, since I was a kid. Every time I heard somebody say daddy, I thought about you. And every time I thought about you, I felt a little pain.

(SYLVIA Looks at SHAREEM as though she is learning this for the first time.)

SHAREEM: Sometimes the pain was so deep that it would hurt my body. One time I was reading this paper about black men and it said that black men who leave their children are finishing the job that the slave masters started. I wondered how a man would do that to his own. Then I started thinking about what you would think of me if you knew me or if you would be proud of me because I could do this or that.

(FRANK tries to talk. SYLVIA and NIKKI look at him, but SHAREEM is unmoved.)

SHAREEM: For a long time, I made sure that everything I was doing, I was doing right because I wanted you to be proud of me when you came back to get me. And yeah, I knew you had another family. I always wondered why you stayed with them but you didn't stay with us.

SYLVIA: Shareem, please!

SHAREEM: I knew Mama had something to do with it but … *(Difficult to say.)* I guess I sort of felt that it was me … so I wanted to prove to you that you were wrong about me. That you could be happy with me. But, you never came to see me. So I just started blocking it all out. I locked it up inside of me and I told myself I would deal with it when it was time.

SYLVIA: Shareem, why don't we give him a chance—

SHAREEM: No, Mama! Let me finish. I want him to hear what I got to say first. *(Pause)* Man, I've had a lot of questions for you over the years. Questions that only you could answer, or should answer. I had to go to Kip and Reggie. They were always there to try and help me fill in your blanks. Only problem was, they were guessing. Do you know how many children are out there like me? All looking for or trying to make some contact with their daddy, so he can fill in some blanks? *(Referring to the books, he has scattered about.)* These books say, that's a damn shame. They say it's a crime when people don't live up to their responsibility. And the law says that people should pay for their crimes. *(Walks toward FRANK.)*

NIKKI: Please don't hurt him, Shareem.

SHAREEM: Why not he hurt me!? He been hurting me for years and nobody pleaded with him to stop. And here I am close to being a father myself. Am I supposed to be like you. *(To FRANK.)* Do I have the right to run off and leave my children and go somewhere else to make other people happy? Huh? *(Pause)* Now, when I take off this gag, I want you to tell me why you didn't stay and take care of me like you were supposed to? And then I want you to tell me what your punishment should be for abandoning me? And don't think I'm playing because I'm ready to carry out your punishment right now! *(Pulls out gun.)*

NIKKI: Oh No! Shareem, No!

SHAREEM: Don't worry. I'm not going to do anything as long as he has the right answers.

SYLVIA: Shareem, Shareem, baby. This is no way to ... to ... fill in your blanks. This is committing a crime.

SHAREEM: And you don't think it was a crime what he did to us! He bought me into the world and left me to fend for myself. That's a crime.

SYLVIA: But Shareem, I was with you.

SHAREEM: *(Anger and pain showing.)* Yeah, and you were catching hell too, feeling pain everyday. I heard you talk about it! I saw you crying about it. *(In FRANKS face.)* IS THAT WHAT A MAN IS SUPPOSED TO DO?

(FRANK tries to speak.)

SYLVIA: But Shareem. How you gonna know if his answers are right or not? Who decides that?

SHAREEM: Me and Nikki because we're the ones getting ready to start a family. And, I want to know from my daddy, what he thinks my responsibilities are. That's what daddies are supposed to teach their sons.

NIKKI: You already know that, Shareem. We've been talking about that for a long time. I know you know what to do.

SHAREEM: That's book knowledge; I want the real thing. And if I have to get it at the point of a gun, I will. *(Points revolver at FRANK.)*

(FRANK falls off the side of the chair onto the floor.)

SYLVIA: Oh no, Shareem! Please don't!

NIKKI: Shareem! Stop! Stop! You know this is not right.

SYLVIA: Shareem. Put that gun away!

SHAREEM: I will, as soon as he gives me the right answers. Now please, put him back in the chair.

(They try and help, but FRANK refuses their help. He stands for a moment looking at SHAREEM. SHAREEM motions for him to sit down. He then motions for NIKKI to take off the gag. FRANK takes a moment to gather himself and then speaks.)

FRANK: *(To SYLVIA)* What did you tell him?

SHAREEM: Hey! I'm asking the questions here.

FRANK: Look, I know that ... and I'm going to answer your questions but I need to get a few blanks filled in myself. *(To SYLVIA.)* So I can say the right things. What did you tell him?

SYLVIA: I told him the truth ... that you didn't want to stay with us.

FRANK: That's a lie and you know it. And, if I'm on trial here today you gonna be on trial too. Tell him the truth or he might as well go ahead and shoot me.

SHAREEM: What truth?

FRANK: That I didn't abandon you.

SHAREEM: *(Pause)* Is that true, Mama?

FRANK: Come on Sylvia fill in that blank. Because it's gonna take both of us to set this story straight. That was not my decision.

SYLVIA: Now there you go again. Talking like it's my fault. It wasn't my fault. You the one decided to leave.

FRANK: Yeah, but I didn't decide to leave because I didn't want to be with him. You know I wanted to be with him.

SHAREEM: Then why didn't you?

FRANK: Come on Sylvia help me out here. Tell this boy—

SHAREEM: I'm your son! And, I'm not a boy. That's what I was when you left me fourteen years ago.

FRANK: No. That's not true. I did not leave you! Tell him Sylvia.

SYLVIA: *(Pause)* Shareem ... your daddy, he tried ... for a while to see you.

SHAREEM: For a while? What are you talking about? What's a while?

FRANK: For years! Tell him, Sylvia, for years.

SHAREEM: For years? What's he talking about, Mama?

SYLVIA: He did try ... for a long while to see you.

SHAREEM: Well, why didn't he get to see me?

FRANK: Yeah, that's the big blank. Why didn't I get to see him, Sylvia?

SYLVIA: *(Angry)* Because, you had another woman. That's why. And you know it!

FRANK: But she didn't have nothing to do with me and my son. That happened before her. Why did you keep me from seeing him?

SYLVIA: Because you put her before us. You started thinking of her before you considered us. You started—

FRANK: That is not true.

SHAREEM: Wait. Let her finish.

SYLVIA: Yes, please, let me finish. This is my blank remember?

FRANK: Yeah, but this is my life, remember?

SHAREEM: Ain't nobody gonna kill you. I'm just gonna punish you like you punished me. Let you feel what it's like to go through life with a handicap. Make your other family sweat a little bit.

FRANK: All I ask is that you know the truth before you pull that trigger.

SYLVIA: He gonna know the truth. Don't you worry about that. *(Pause)* Shareem, you can untie him. He ain't going nowhere.

NIKKI: Yeah, Shareem. Untie him. I think it would be better that way. And Shareem. Please give me my gun. *(Quietly, to SHAREEM.)* Anyway, it ain't got no bullets in it.

SHAREEM: Yes there is. I put them in myself.

(After a moment, SHAREEM unties FRANK and they all sit in silence for a long while. SHAREEM looks at his mother.)

SYLVIA: Well ... here we are. A family gathering after all these years.

SHAREEM: What happened Mama?

SYLVIA: Well, to make a long story short, there I was, a single mother with child. Now don't that sound just like your books? *(Pause)* Shareem, I don't have any way to defend myself. Any answer is gonna sound stupid. The only thing I can tell you is that, at the time, I had no idea, what-so-ever, about what was a good decision or a bad one. I was so full of hate and anger, I just wanted him out of my life and I looked at you as mine. So I made that decision for you. And then, after a while it was too late. I lost track of him and I guess, he lost track of me.

FRANK: No I didn't. I knew where you were. I've always known where you were.

NIKKI: Then why didn't you come looking for him? How come—

FRANK: Just hold on a minute, I'm gonna tell him. *(To SHAREEM.)* Son, I guess, in all rights, you should hurt me. But it would just be junk piled on top of junk.

SHAREEM: Just tell me why you didn't come to see me.

SYLVIA: Because I wouldn't let him.

NIKKI: But, Why?

SYLVIA: I don't know. Pride ... I guess.

FRANK: Would you all listen to me please! I need to get this out.

NIKKI: Go ahead, I'm sorry.

FRANK: I didn't come because I was a fool, an ignorant, stupid fool. And for a long time, I was afraid ...

SHAREEM: Afraid of what?

FRANK: *(Pause)* That you ... wouldn't want me ... so why try. I use to ask my mother about you. She always knew where you were. My mother didn't think much of me, or men for that matter, and she told me that I should leave you alone. She said you and your mother were doing fine and that I should just take care of myself and try to do right by my other family.

SHAREEM: But what about us? We were your family too.

FRANK: I know that now, but I didn't feel like that then.

SHAREEM: Well what did you feel? That's what I need to know.

FRANK: *(Long pause)* I didn't feel nuthin'. That's what the problem was. I didn't know what to feel. I just thought that was the way it was. Nobody was telling me or showing me that it was supposed to be any different. You say you saw all the kids, well I saw all the men.

SHAREEM: But you stayed with your other family. Why?

FRANK: Because I started looking around me and I could see that if I continued to think and feel like I was, I wouldn't have anything good in life. So I decided to try it again. But I knew I had to do a better job, you know get it right.

SHAREEM: But you didn't want to do right by me?

FRANK: You never left my mind. You've been burning inside of me for a long time. I knew that this day was coming. I knew I had to see you. So when your partners came to get me, I came along, almost willingly, because I knew it was time. Way pass time. So you see, I'm glad to see you ... you're the only person that can erase my pain. So I'm ready for whatever you gonna do.

(SHAREEM slowly walks toward his father. FRANK sees the gun in his hand but does not show any fear.)

SHAREEM: You got ten seconds to tell me why I shouldn't hurt you like you hurt us.

SYLVIA: No Shareem. If you hurt him you might as well hurt me.

SHAREEM: But you stayed with me. He didn't.

FRANK: I know I didn't but if you hurt me that would make you just like me and you got me here—you say—so I can fill in the blanks. So here it is.

SHAREEM: Go ahead.

(NIKKI walks over to stand with SHAREEM.)

FRANK: When you become a man and I mean a real man, you have to face the mistakes you make. And yeah, you too will make some mistakes. Now, I know that we can't go back to the way things were. But this is one fire that we can put out, but it means that you have to help me do it. Because you know I was wrong and I know I was wrong but we've got to work together to make it right.

SYLVIA: And I know I was wrong.

FRANK: So what we got to do is to rebuild. That's what a lot of people do after a bad fire. They rebuild.

SHAREEM: Rebuild what?

FRANK: *(FRANK finds these words hard to say.)* Rebuild our family.

SHAREEM: But you've got another family.

FRANK: No. That was my first mistake. You're still my family. I've just got to learn how to take care of it. But if you hurt me, you are gonna make it damned hard for us to do what we got to do. And you're also gonna have to figure out what to tell your son—or are you planning on doing the same thing to him.

NIKKI: Or our daughter.

SYLVIA: Come on Shareem. We can do this.

(SHAREEM stands in the middle of the floor with the gun at his side. After a moment he gives the gun to NIKKI.)

SYLVIA: Thank you Shareem. *(She goes to him and gives him a long hug.)*

FRANK: *(Pause)* Can you please untie my hands. These ropes are killing me.

NIKKI: Okay Shareem?

(SHAREEM nods yes and NIKKI unties his hands.)

SYLVIA: For a minute there I thought we were gonna have some of that domestic violence up in here like your books be talking about. But instead we got us another chance. Now all we have to do is figure out how to make it work.

FRANK: Don't worry about that, I've been thinking about this for a long time. I got a few ideas about how to fill in those blanks too. But there is one blank that I can't fill in.

SYLVIA: What's that?

(FRANK looks at SHAREEM who is standing with NIKKI.)

FRANK: Is my son willing to work with me?

SHAREEM: *(Long Pause)* Sure … it beats my plan all to hell.

NIKKI: Shareem this gun doesn't have any bullets in it.

(Black Out)

(The End)

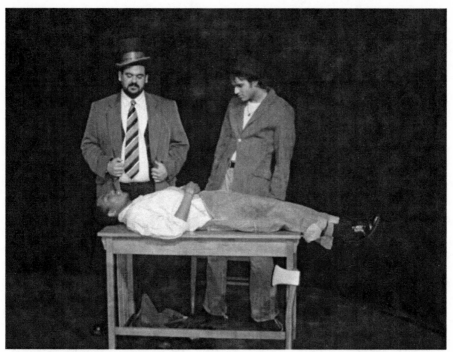

Mike Holmes as DOC, Arjin Gupta as LEX and Eric Lockley (on table) as JACK in JACK in The Riant Theatre's Strawberry One-Act Festival Winter 2008 at The American Theater of Actors in NYC

JACK

By Daren Taylor

Daren Taylor is a recent graduate of NYU's Tisch School of the Arts Drama department. During his previous travels through Europe and Asia, he began to develop plays about the fantasy worlds he saw around him. Obsessed with mythology, and it's affects on the society which created it, most of Daren's plays deal with people coming into conflict with their beliefs. He has previously written *What a Man!*, *Exodus*, and *What Would Dad Do? Jack* is his first play to receive a full production.

Jack made its New York City debut on February 16, 2008 at the American Theatre of Actors. It was a semi-finalist in The Riant Theatre's Winter 2008 Strawberry One-Act Festival with the following cast, in order of appearance (For this production, all townspeople were played by women):

JACK	Eric Lockley
MA	Nicole Rose
DOC	Mike Holmes
HOODED FIGURE	Aaron Sparks
WOMAN 1	Christiamilda Correa
WOMAN 2	Kate Moran
WOMAN 3	Rajeeyah Finnie
LEX	Rajeeyah Finnie
JIMMY	Arjin Gupta
BILL	Aaron Sparks

The play was directed by Daren Taylor.

CAST OF CHARACTERS

JACK, male, 14-18. Very naïve and gullible, but carefree. Wants nothing more to enjoy life. He loves both his sister and mother very much.

MA, female 30-40s. Beaten down by the hardships of a poor existence. Very distrusting of men, and relies on her own strength to get by. She is very close to giving it all up.

DOC, male, mid to lat 30s. The town doctor. Everyone in the town took in the mysterious character when he showed up in town a year ago. He has been very helpful, and as a result, makes a living off other people's hard work.

BILL, male, early 30s. Friend of Doc.

LEX, female, early 30s. Friend of Doc.

JIMMY, Male, early 30s. Friend of Doc.

MAN 1, male, any age. Townsperson.

MAN 2, male, any age. Townsperson.

WOMAN 1, female, any age. Townsperson.

HOODED FIGURE, a hooded figure.

SCENE 1

(Jack's house. Very messy run down home. In the darkness JACK is posing. It is hard to discern what he is doing. But we can hear him humming a song. Lights up as MA runs on stage looking for JACK, calling his name, when he notices his mother, he immediately stops.)

MA: What was you doing boy?

JACK: I … I was praying momma.

MA: You was what?

JACK: P … praying?

MA: Where you get that from?

JACK: What momma?

MA: That! The idea of praying?

JACK: Well … Jill

MA: Ain't no prayin' in this house boy! I told your sister that, now I'm telling you that.

JACK: I know momma, but today's the day.

MA: You killed your sister. So you feeling guilty for it. That why you doing that stuff in this house?

JACK: Momma … aint no one around. We don't have to pretend. God don't—

MA: Ain't no such thing as God boy! And I ain't pretending. Everyone in the town knows you—

JACK: But you know the truth momma. You know that I didn't push her, she just—

MA: Enough! I told you not to mention her in the first place. So no need to be talking about it, and there definitely ain't no reason for you to be praying about it. Have you lost your mind boy?

JACK: No momma, I was just trying to honor her memory.

MA: Honor!?!? Ha. If you had any honor, you wouldn't have come back. You'd have killed yourself on that hill along with your sister. Useless ... and now we struggling to make ends meet.

JACK: I know momma. I'm not Jill, but I'm trying ...

MA: Not hard enough! We in debt boy, and you're prayin' ain't help us get out of it.

JACK: I'm sorry momma. I'll try harder ... I love you.

MA: What I tell you about that? We don't got time for that Jack. Love don't stop us from getting sick, love don't keep us fed, and love don't pay for this house. This aint some fantasy world boy. There are bills to pay. We can't be wastin' our time believing in something we can't put our five senses on. Because your idiot daddy ran off chasing some fantasy, we left here in all kinds of debt. It done cost me my baby, and it done left me here stuck with you. You just like your daddy-ain't worth the space you take up. So while you sittin' there prayin' and lovin', and all that foolishness, how we gonna survive Jack? You know I can only do but so much. When you gonna grow up and be a man and support this family Jack?

JACK: I don't know momma.

MA: I know you don't. So stop all that foolishness and do as I told you.

JACK: But why we need to sell off the cow, what happened to all the money that Jill had made—

MA: That ain't none of your concern. I told you to go and sell that cow and that's what you better do.

JACK: But don't we need the food more? I mean, with the famine and all—

MA: There you go thinking, again. Instead of thinking, you need to start doin'!

JACK: Yes momma. I'm sorry for thinking ... I love—

MA: Git! *(Blackout.)*

SCENE 2

(The road. JACK is walking and he notices a HOODED FIGURE standing there.)

JACK: Hello friend. Not many people at the market today. *(Silence.)* Yeah ... no one wanted to buy my cow. Not even for cheap. Momma's gonna be upset. *(Silence.)* I can't go back empty handed. Maybe you got something? Anything would be better than nothing, right? *(Silence. HOODED FIGURE holds out his hands. There are three seeds.)* What's that? Seeds? You think momma would be happy with seeds? But it's only three friends. Not much you can do with three seeds. I'm not stupid. *(Silence.)* Unless you was selling magic seeds. That way, you wouldn't need so many and you'd get a good harvest! That way, we could not only eat, but sell the extra and make some money! Wow, I'll take em. *(Stranger holds out other hand, and accepts the cow.)* Thanks friend, momma will be happy about this. Magic seeds! What's your name friend? *(The lights flicker. Blackout. Lights up, the stranger is gone.)* Uh oh. That's not good. I hope that wasn't a trick or nothing. Darn it! It probably was. Stupid Jack! These seeds aint magic. *(He examines the seeds.)* And I just gave away a good cow for nothing. *(He throws the seeds offstage.)* Oh Jill, you wouldn't have fallen for a stupid trick like that would you? You were a lot smarter than me. I sure wish you were still here. I miss you … you used to always take care of me. I wish you still could. *(JACK looks around, and begins to try and pray and begins to kneel. As soon as he starts humming, there is a huge rumbling sound and the ground shakes. It stops. He looks offstage.)* What in God's name is that? *(Looking up.)* Is that … a giant beanstalk? Those seeds were magic! Did you do this Jill? Is you lookin' after me from heaven? Is this your way of helping me after I messed up? Guess there's only one way to find out. Next stop, up! *(He rushes offstage. Blackout.)*

SCENE 3
(Jack's house. MA is cleaning the house. The door bursts open and a disheveled JACK is standing in the doorway. MA jumps up and runs towards the door.)

MA: Where have you been boy? *(Silence.)* You've been gone for 6 days. People was saying that you ran away, but I knew you wasn't bright enough to do something stupid like that. I thought I told you—*(JACK falls to the floor.)* Jack? Jack! What's wrong baby? What happened to you? Did somebody do this to you? Who did this to you? *(He pulls out a large piece of gold.)* What is this? Where did you get this? *(He faints.)* Oh … help! Somebody help!!

SCENE 4
(Doc Smith's house/practice. Jack is laying on the table while Doc and Ma are talking.)

MA: And then he wanders back in holdin this. *(Shows him the golden nugget. DOC takes it and examines it. He stops paying attention to MA.)* I figured you bein' the well traveled man that you are, you'd be able to tell me what it is that my son got beat up for. *(Pause)* Doc Smith?
DOC: Yes, sorry. Where did you say he got this from?

MA: I don't know. The boy ain't bright enough to have stolen it from somebody. Unless they was dumber than him, and that'd be a stretch. *(They both laugh, and have a moment.)* You sure is lookin' at it funny, is it worth anything?

DOC: Hm? Oh, this thing? It's not worth nothing ma'am. This is just some old stone that the kids use to play all sorts of games with. He must have gone to some other town and gotten it from another kid. That's probably why he was gone so long. Nothing special about this … nothing.

MA: Well I'm sorry to be wasting your time … um, we kinda short on money right now, and since ain't nothing really wrong with my boy, could we just—

DOC: *(Getting closer to her.)* Oh this wasn't a wasted trip ma'am. I'm always glad to see you. And as for this thing, are you sure he didn't say anything about where he got it? Looks like he went to an awful lot of trouble to get it …

MA: You more concerned with that old thing, or my boy doctor?

DOC: It's just that, if I could have this old thing, then maybe I could wave the fees for the visit. I'd really appreciate it. It reminds me of something from my childhood, and it has a very high value to me. I'm a bit of a sucker for … nostalgia. *(A clock chimes and JACK suddenly jumps up looking like a wild beast.)* Woah there son. Calm down. We were just—*(DOC goes to touch him, but JACK jerks away.)* Relax. You are at my office because you were attacked, and you fainted. Your poor mother was worried about you, and she brought you here. See.

MA: You just had a run in with some bullies boy, no reason to get all upset and disrupt the good doctors home. *(JACK fervently shakes his head no.)*

DOC: It's ok son, boys get beat up all the time. It's a part of growing up. Believe it or not, I was once a scrawny little nothing like you, and I would get picked on all the time. *(DOC and MA laugh. DOC goes to put his hand on JACK'S shoulder, JACK grabs a weapon and backs away from DOC.)*

MA: Put that down boy! What's gotten into you. *(To DOC)* I swear, I didn't raise him like this.

JACK: I seen him ma.

MA: What?

JACK: I seen him. I … I spoke to him.

MA: Spoke to who?

JACK: To God momma. I spoke to God. I did something stupid momma and I'm real sorry, but God took care of me … of us.

MA: What did you do boy?

JACK: I didn't sell the cow. Instead I bought these holy seeds from an angel.

DOC: Angel? *(Jack looks at Doc and growls.)*

MA: What are you talking about Jack?

JACK: I bought these holy seeds from an angel, and they took me to God. He must have heard my prayers, or Jill told him that we was needing help—

MA: Don't!

JACK: No momma, she looking out for us. Up there. When she would pray, she would always look up to the sky. She must have told God I wanted to see him. That's why he sent an angel, that's why he let me talk to him. That's why he wanted to help us.

MA: Help how Jack?

JACK: I told God everything. About how poor we was, about how I'm no good, even about how Jill—

MA: I said leave her out of this!

JACK: Forgive me, but God said that he can help us. Us momma! Even after all the bad we done done. Just like the old stories. Then he gave me a gift and said that this would take care of our problems. A gift from God momma. It's gonna take care of all our ... *(Searches his pockets.)* Where is it? He told me not to let it out of my sight. Where is it!?

DOC: You mean this worthless thing? *(Pulls out the golden egg.)*

JACK: *(Lunging and swiping at DOC.)* Give it back!

MA: No Jack, don't!

DOC: Yes Jack, calm down before ... someone gets hurt.

JACK: You got no right holding that. That belongs to us.

MA: Never you mind boy. That thing is useless—

JACK: No it ain't! It's what you've always wanted momma. I know you don't do it in public, but it's what you've been praying for. God said you could be rich with that. We wouldn't have to worry about money or working ever again. We could go back to how we used to be ... when you was happy.

MA: *(Looking from DOC to JACK)* I don't pray you stupid idiot! I am a law abiding town folk. And if god was gonna answer anything, then he would have answered me a long time ago when I said I wanted Jill back in exchange for you.

JACK: Momma ... *(He curls into a ball and sits on the floor, crying.)*

DOC: Clearly the boy is delusional. Ma'am, if you could just leave while I try to cure him. Free of charge of course. This nonsense about god aint good for no one. I wouldn't want to see you or your boy taken by the sheriff.

MA: You are so considerate doctor. Are you sure you can cure him?

DOC: Don't you worry about that ma'am, I'm proficient in all types of healin'.

MA: Thank you. *(She exits.)*

DOC: OK son. Man to man, lets talk about—

JACK: *(Jumping back up)* Give it back.

DOC: Maybe …

JACK: It's mine.

DOC: Well right now, it's in my hands. So technically it's mine. *(JACK strikes a strange pose, and looks to the sky and begins to hum the song from beginning under his breath.)*

What you doing boy?

JACK: Prayin'.

DOC: *(He laughs.)* I seen a lot of foolishness in my time boy, but never have I seen somebody prayin'. Who you prayin' to son? Don't you know god don't exist no more. He quit on us a long time ago. *(JACK continues.)* I'm pretty new around these parts, but ain't you the boy that went coocoo after he threw himself down that hill after killing his sister? Don't the kids sing "Jack and Jill went up the hill to fetch a pail of water, Jack got pissed, and pushed his sis and jumped down right after." That fall must have messed up your noodle if you think you done seen god—*(JACK lunges at DOC with his weapon trying to kill him. The DOC quickly pulls a gun out of one of his drawers. JACK freezes in place.)* But I see you got some sense in you. Now sit! *(JACK sits.)* Good, I knew we could have a civilized conversation. *(DOC sits, still point the gun.)* Ok? Where did you get this?

JACK: From God. He said it was a gift for me and my family.

DOC: Ok. And this … god, what did he look like?

JACK: Big … real big.

DOC: And where did he get this golden egg from?

JACK: It's gold? That's what it looks like? Of course!

DOC: Where, boy.

JACK: From a chicken. *(Pause.)*

DOC: A chicken? A chicken laid a golden egg?

JACK: God works in mysterious ways.

DOC: And where did you meet god?

JACK: God told me not to tell anyone where I planted it—

DOC: Planted? What do you mean?

JACK: Nothing …

DOC: I asked you a question. *(JACK shakes his head no, DOC puts the gun in his face.)*

JACK: I ain't afraid of you.

DOC: You should be. *(Pause.)*

You got one more chance boy. I could kill you right now and tell everyone in town it was a "medical accident." People wouldn't miss you. Hell, they'd probably thank me for getting rid of you. So tell me where you got this gold from.

JACK: No. *(Pause, as the DOC considers his options.)*

DOC: Fine. But I keep this. I need to make sure this isn't some sort of trick. And when I'm done with it, your Ma and I gonna decide what to do with it. Now git. *(JACK begins to exit.)* And don't you go telling nobody about this. People gonna think you crazy, and I don't need you getting hurt ... your momma wouldn't never forgive me. *(Door slams.)*

SCENE 5

(Town square with various vendors and workers. JACK is standing on top of a crate preaching to whoever will listen. He is wearing a dirty hooded cloak, and he has three dots on his forehead in the shape of a triangle. There are a few people listening.)

JACK: Who's hungry? Who's starving? Who's cold, or sick, or any of those things? Well I found a way to beat them things. You wanna know how? God ...

MAN 1: What you say boy?

JACK: I know it's been outlawed, but he's real. I've seen him.

WOMAN 1: What you mean you seen him?

JACK: I prayed—*(People gasp.)* no, no. It's ok. I prayed and he answered. I looked to the sky and I asked for his help.

MAN 1: What you look to the sky for, ain't nothing up there for us.

WOMAN 1: I ain't got no time to be keeping my head in the clouds. I gotta work to keep my family alive.

JACK: But if we just raised our heads.

MAN 1: She's right. If you got time to be looking up, then you got time to be working with the rest of us. I'm too busy making my livelihood to be worried about anything else. Ya lazy kid.

JACK: But we don't have to live in poverty no more. We don't have to wallow around in the mud for the rest of our lives. We have hope ... in God. He ain't no myth, I seen him. He is kind and full of mercy, just like we've been told.

MAN 1: Where in the hell did you meet God? The watering hole? *(Laughter.)*

JACK: He told me not to tell no one, but just look to the sky—*(More laughter.)*

WOMAN 1: How you get so beat up? Did God do that to you?

MAN 1: I heard he got beat up by some bullies from another town. They must have messed his brains up if he thinks he's seeing God. *(Even more laughter.)*

JACK: No, I got this when I fell!

WOMAN 1: Fell from where? From up? *(Laughter.)*

JACK: I can't say ...

MAN 1: Let's recap. All you've told us was that you can't tell us nothing. *(Laughter)*

WOMAN 1: That family really went to hell once the sister died. What was her name?

MAN 1: Jill. Beautiful girl. Too bad about her.

WOMAN 1: Yeah, she was a sweet girl. Beautiful voice. Real smart too.

MAN 1: She was always studying with that scholar over by them fields. Giving her all sorts of books and such.

WOMAN 1: Then her brother went and killed her.

MAN 1: I would have killed my sister too if I found out she was a prostitute.

WOMAN 1: No! She was not.

MAN 1: Sure as the cow moos. The momma was whoring her out so she could live the good life. That's how she met that smart fella. Brother found out and threw her down Flatland Hill. Then the sicko threw himself down for the hell of it.

WOMAN 1: Sad really.

MAN 1: Yeah it is. *(They begin to exit.)*

JACK: No, don't leave. He's real! There's hope. He hasn't left us yet.

WOMAN 1: Oh yeah? So where's he been the last 50 years while we been suffering? On vacation? *(Laughter.)*

MAN 1: You keep them fairy tails up, you gonna cause a lot of trouble around here kid.

(All exit but JACK. Blackout.)

SCENE 6

(Jack's house. DOC and MA sit, drinking tea.)

MA: Gold?

DOC: Yes.

MA: Well where is it? We could—

DOC: I had to send it to a friend to examine it. He sent me a post letting me know that it's real. Don't worry, we can trust him.

MA: Do you know what this means? I can finally get out of this place. This poverty, this sick, disgusting place. I can put it behind me ...

DOC: We'll I had other arrangements.

MA: Well ... I know it was you who found out what it was doctor, so it is only fair that we split it 50-50—

DOC: That's not what I meant.

MA: Well say what you mean doctor. I don't got all day.

DOC: What I meant was that we don't split it. 100% goes to us.

MA: Us? What you meaning doctor?

DOC: I mean you and I run away ... together.

MA: I done had my fill of men in my life. You all can't be trusted as far as you can spit.

DOC: I'm not sayin' you need me, what I'm saying is ... I want you. I want to take care of you. Treat you like you ain't never been treated. I know it ain't easy gettin' along in a place like this. I mean, without no man to help. You don't get no respect. People don't think you women can do for yourselves like us men, but I see the type of strong woman that you are, and I respect that. I wanna give you the life you deserve. The one you always should have had. One without all these worries, where you can finally be free.

MA: You ... you mean that?

DOC: Would I be here speaking what I'm speaking if I didn't?

MA: You sure talk pretty, and I'm not saying that I trust you. But how we gonna make this happen?

DOC: Well, that little piece ain't enough to carry us for the rest of our lives. We need more, and Jack is the only one who can get it for us.

MA: He ain't gonna tell me where it is.

DOC: We can't let him get in the way of our happiness. You gotta find a way to get it out of him. The sooner you can get it out of him, the sooner we can get rid of all our cares and start over. And I can start earning your trust ... *(He kisses her. JACK enters.)*

JACK: Get out.

DOC: Good day to you too Jack. I'll talk to you later ma'am. *(DOC exits.)*

JACK: What was he doing here?

MA: We was discussing what to do with what you found.

JACK: But God intended that—

MA: How many times I'm gonna have to tell you "God" don't exist.

JACK: But it's true momma. I met him. He was big, and kind, and there was this song ...

MA: Even if you did meet someone that was like that, what makes you think it was god boy?

JACK: Cause the song was Jill's song momma. The one she used when she was prayin'. It was the same song, so I knew it was her ... lookin' out for us. *(Long pause.)*

MA: I told you before—and I ain't telling you again. God don't exist. If he did, why he take Jill in the first place? Why this whole area ain't hardly got no food? Why we all dying Jack? What kind of god would do that? Why don't he help us?

JACK: But we got the gold ma, he wants to help.

MA: The doctor said that wasn't even no gold. Said it was—

JACK: You letting that evil doctor trick you. God—*(She slaps him.)*

MA: I don't need no imaginary friend to help me. He done had plenty of opportunities to help, and he didn't. I got scars on top of scars on my heart, waiting for something good to happen. Waiting for others to do good by me. Jill's cheatin' father, your lazy runaway father. Waiting for something to happen. How long I'm supposed to wait for this miracle Jack? I don't see no god, and you may want to believe that you did boy, but you ain't been right since Jill ... anyway, you think I can wait on him to help me out when he feels like it? I can't keep it together no longer Jack. They gonna take the house next week cause I can't pay for it. Is your god gonna help me before then? Cause I know you ain't. I been telling you for years to be a man. Take some responsibility. I guess I should have been more specific, cause you are turning into a man ... your father. He ain't never understand money don't grow on trees and apparently neither do you. I need support here and now, and maybe the good doctor is gonna help me. Maybe he's different than the others. Maybe not. But I'd rather take that chance than waiting for your God that hasn't done me right since I can remember. I can't wait no longer ... *(JACK goes offstage. He re-enters with a bag and makes for the front door.)* Where you going with that bag boy?

JACK: Nowhere momma.

MA: Don't lie to me. You planning on running away? You done turned coward like your father boy? You gonna be just like all the others.

JACK: I love you momma.

MA: What?

JACK: I'm gonna finally take care of you momma. I'm gonna show you that you don't need no one else, especially not no evil doctor ... cause God is there for us. He won't try and trick us like other greedy people. And no matter what you say, he ain't gonna leave us. I'll be back, momma, I promise. *(He exits. MA stands there with a huge grin on her face. Beat. She runs out the house after him.)*

SCENE 7

(Doc's office. He enters while 3 others are taking inventory and clearing out the office.)

DOC: All the waiting done paid off.

BILL: Ain't no way in hell.

LEX: Really?

DOC: We been squattin in this town long enough. And now we bout to get our biggest pay day ever.

JIMMY: Hot damn!

DOC: So pack it up! No telling how long he's gonna be up there. We got enough bags?

LEX: Enough to fill up six times over.

DOC: We gonna hit this place once, and once only. Most important thing is the chicken. After we get that, fill up with whatever other valuables we find and then cut out. Jimmy, you grab the ax. Bill, you gonna be on lookout while me and Lex loot away. Soon as we get back, Jimmy, cut that thing down.

LEX: Don't want nobody gitting rich off our scheme.

DOC: Or anything following us back down. We don't got no time for reconnaissance, so we gotta do this quick and clean.

BILL: Are you all crazy!?

ALL: What?

BILL: Imma give you three reasons why this is a bad idea.

JIMMY: Oh come off it Bill.

BILL: One, we goin' in blind

LEX: Since when you turn chicken?

BILL: Two, there could be a pissed off who-knows-what up there. The boy said it was huge—

JIMMY: The kid's cracked more times than your old lady's tea set.

BILL: And three, what if—

DOC: Don't say it.

BILL: Why not? We all thinking it Smith! They just too scared to say it.

JIMMY: Say what?

BILL: Ok, Jimmy's too stupid … but I ain't scared.

DOC: Really? Then speak your mind pal.

BILL: What if the boy is right?

LEX: Right about what? *(Pause.)* About god being up there?

BILL: Yes. *(LEX and JIMMY laugh hysterically.)*

JIMMY: And I'm the stupid one? You actually think that boy has been seeing God?

BILL: Then what the hell's up there Jimmy? Where in the world did he get gold from? Gold ain't been seen in this land for hundreds of years. People think it's some kinda fairytale like Rapunzel or Rumpelstiltskin. There ain't no place for him to get it from but—

LEX: God? You done turned fool Bill. You believe this little dirt rat is actually talking to god?

DOC: *(Cleaning his gun.)* Don't matter. We going up and finding out soon as Jack comes back down.

BILL: But—

DOC: Enough. I let you say your piece out of respect for our friendship. But I ain't gonna take this back talk. We all got the plan, and we gonna execute it.

BILL: What you gonna do is execute a kid Smith!

JIMMY: Calm down buddy.

BILL: I ain't gonna calm down! I don't care how poor we is, or how bad it's been, we done got greedy Jimmy. We done lost the value of life. Is gold worth someone's life? Especially a kids? What in God's name—*(Gunshot. BILL falls to the floor dead.)*

DOC: Yes. *(He goes over to BILL's body, takes his gun and tosses it to JIMMY. Both he and LEX are in shock.)* Now you on guard duty and responsible for cutting it down. Think you can handle that?

JIMMY: Yeah Smith ... I can.

DOC: Good. Glad I can count on you.

LEX: But ... Bill, he was—

DOC: *(Grabbing LEX.)* Ain't no way in hell or heaven I'm gonna stay in this shit hole any longer than I have. I been wallowing in the mud so damn long, I'm used to the coat of filth I'm wearing. Man wasn't meant to live like this, especially when there's people out there living rich and carefree lives. What? They deserve it more than you or me Lex? Jimmy? If god is up there, then I'm gonna put a bullet between his eyes too, for picking favorites. We don't deserve this. I'm a good man who just wants what he deserves. And no real man would except this kind of life, and I ain't gonna let nobody get in my way neither. Nobody. Maybe god just needs to see how serious we are about this. Hell, we might even get up there and he just gives us everything. Ain't gonna stop me from making him dead though. But ... it's the thought that counts ... if he even exists. *(He laughs.)*

LEX: *(Closing BILL'S eyes.)* What about his family?

DOC: We'll send his widow some of our a cut of the profit. How much gold does it take to make someone forget? *(Pause.)* Guess we gonna find out. *(To LEX.)* And, never you mind about his family. You need to worry about ours. *(He kisses her. In bursts MA.)*

MA: So what do we do ... now.

LEX: Who are you old lady?

MA: I ... well I'm ... but I thought—

LEX: Well whatever you thought, I'm sure you're mistaken.

DOC: Now wait a minute Lex, I'd like to hear her out. Ma'am, please.

MA: I thought ... you said we was gonna be together. The two of us. All those plans you made about us getting out.

LEX: You was planning things behind my back? As your wife—

MA: You're married?

DOC: Now darling. It was all part of a larger plan. I had to subject myself to cooing this old sack so I could make a better future for us.

MA: Sack?

LEX: But you never said—

DOC: And it done paid off right? We bout to become richer than we ever dreamed. Richer than ... god himself! *(He laughs.)*

MA: What about me? What about the dreams I believe in now?

LEX: What is it a slut like you dreams about? Sucking another man dry until he runs away? Like they say you did to your first husband? Or the second? Or maybe like—

MA: Shut your mouth.

LEX: Oh, looks like she has some life in her yet.

MA: *(To Doc.)* But I thought you was different. I thought you loved—

LEX: Ha! You don't know what love is lady. I'm sorry to tell ya, but that yearning between your legs ain't love. Ask your daughter about that. That's the reason she killed herself right, cause you made her—*(MA rushes at LEX, LEX slaps her and she falls to the ground. She pulls out her gun and points it at her.)* Please do that again. I'm looking for a reason to kill you.

DOC: Calm down Lex, she ain't worth it. Ma'am, take my advice: if your boy survives this mess, I suggest you send some of your love that way. Instead of blaming him for your past mistakes. And if you so happen to have another daughter, kill her while she's young. Cause you ain't fit to bring one up. Good day ma'am. *(MA is left sitting on the floor. Lights begin to fade. Light bump back up as JACK enters.)*

JACK: I knew you'd probably be here momma. We don't need him no more. *(He dumps his sack full of gold on the table.)* See?

MA: I was wrong Jack ... again. Just like your daddy.

JACK: But we don't need them no more. Look momma, I'm providing for us. Just like you always wanted. Now we can be happy again.

MA: Why do they always fill you up with their dreams. Make you believe in them, and then snatch em away ...

JACK: But I love you momma. Don't that count for something?

MA: It's cause of her. There's always something getting in the way. Always taking what belongs to me. Taking my dreams away ...

JACK: What are you talking about momma.

MA: They went up the stalk Jack. They gonna steal from god.

JACK: No! How did they find it?

MA: I ... it don't matter. We gotta stop them. We can't let them get away.

JACK: God told me not to tell anyone about how to get up there. He's gonna be mad momma. Real mad.

MA: Then go stop them boy! Do something useful instead of standing here talking about it. I'm gonna go get the town folk. We can't let thieves get away with what's ours … we can't.

JACK: You're right momma. Those thieves won't get away with this. I'm gonna stop em. *(He runs out.)*

MA: She won't get away with this. And then it'll be just him and me … *(Blackout.)*

SCENE 8

(The road near the stalk. JIMMY is keeping watch with the gun and the ax. JACK enters.)

JIMMY: Hey son, keep it moving. Nothing to see here. *(JACK doesn't move.)* Hey, scat kid. I don't wanna hurt you, but if I gotta … *(We hear a commotion offstage. It's MA and the townsfolk. While JIMMY looks away, JACK rushes him and wrestles the gun away from him. He takes a rock and bashes him in the head, knocking Jimmy out. He leaves the gun on ground and takes the ax. In comes MA and three others.)*

MAN 1: Is it really up there?

MAN 2: The gold?

MA: All of it is up there.

WOMAN 1: How did we never see this before?

MAN 1: That kid was right. All we had to do was look up …

JACK: I stopped him momma, just like you said.

MA: Did anyone come down yet?

JACK: Nope. I was quick. Now I'm gonna cut it down so that they can't come back. Let God deal with them.

MAN 1: *(Grabbing Jack.)* Are you crazy boy? This is a chance of a lifetime. We gotta get up there and fill our pockets.

MA: That's not part of the deal. We just supposed to capture—

MAN 2: Why would we blow an opportunity like this? Gold? Actual gold? We'll be set for life after we get back down. We won't have to be hungry no more!

MA: No, that's not part of the deal.

WOMAN 1: You deal with your own problems. This is our chance to be rich.

JACK: No!

ALL: What?

JACK: No! God doesn't give to greedy people. He only gives to those who seek him humbly.

MAN 2: Shut up kid. Get out of our way.

JACK: No. It wasn't supposed to be like this. We were supposed to accept God's gifts, not try to steal from him. This is all my fault, I've brought evil on us all. If we keep this up, our greed is gonna destroy us. And since I started it, I gotta fix it. *(He runs offstage and we hear chopping sounds.)*

WOMAN 1: Idiot! Stop it. Don't make us hurt you.

MAN 1: He's gonna ruin us. This is our one chance and he's gonna take it from us. *(MA throws a rock. Then another.)*

MA: No Jack stop. Not yet. Not yet! *(Now the others join in throwing rocks. Pelting JACK offstage. He begins to hum the song from the beginning. The chopping continues. We hear a thud, and out runs DOC. MA sees him, and runs to him.)*

MA: Stop them! Stop them, they're gonna kill him! He don't deserve this.

DOC: Where is she? Where is she?

MA: Who cares. Stop them from killing my son.

DOC: We got separated. That infernal music got in our heads and made things all fuzzy. Then that thing started chasing us. Did she make it back? Did she at least throw the sack down?

MA: They're killing my son, and all you can think about is gold?

DOC: Is that what you want? Gold? *(Digging in his pockets.)* Here, that should take care of your problems.

MA: You selfish son of a bitch … *(Yelling to the mob.)* Over here! This is one of them. Check his bag, there's gold in it.

MAN 1: Get him.

DOC: Wait, wait. Where is she—*(The mob stops pelting JACK and mauls DOC. He tries to pull out his gun, but they are too much for him. They over power him and beat him to death. Stealing all his possessions. JACK stumbles out and dies in MA'S arms. She wails in pain.)*

MA: Not you too. I've lost both my children because of my selfishness. I'm sorry Jack. I'm so sorry. I love you baby. *(More people run on stage.)*

MAN 1: There really is gold. So there must be more up there.

WOMAN 1: Let's go! *(The mob runs off stage and begins to climb the stalk. We hear it begin to creak as MA delivers her final speech.)*

MA: *(Looking up.)* I done done a lot of wrong in this lifetime God, and I understand that I gotta pay for it. But if you must take me … take me where you took him. Please God … please. I love him. *(We hear a break, screams, and a crash. Blackout.)*

(End of Play)

Susan Perry as LANA and Dustin Charles as FRANCES
in MARKED in The Riant Theatre's Strawberry One-Act Festival Winter 2008
at The American Theater of Actors in NYC

MARKED

By Cassandra Lewis

Cassandra Lewis is a writer whose work has been published in *The Stanford Social Innovation Review, Word Riot, Expatica*, and she has received numerous reporting credits in the *Village Voice*. Seven of her other plays have been performed in San Francisco and Chicago. Her performing arts background includes training from The Studio Theatre in Washington DC, The Ballet Academy of Northern Virginia, and Stella Adler Studio of Acting in New York. She earned an MFA in Writing from New College of California and spent the summer of 2006 in Dublin completing the University of Iowa's Irish Writing Program. Cassandra is a member of The Dramatists Guild and PEN USA.

Marked made its debut in New York City on February 16, 2008 at The American Theatre of Actors in the Chernuchin Theatre. It was a finalist in the Winter 2008 Strawberry One-Act Festival. Vanessa Lozano was nominated for Best Director and Suzan Perry was nominated for Best Actress. The cast, in order of appearance, was as follows:

LANA   Suzan Perry
FRANCIS   Dustin Charles

The play was directed by Vanessa Lozano.

CAST OF CHARACTERS

LANA, a mother who has worried herself into oblivion over the span of her life, 53 years. Despite her eccentric behavior, she is eloquent and determined to "survive" by sustaining her unique logic.
FRANCIS, an aspiring artist in his thirties who has a thing for doctors. Aesthetics are important to him, even in terms of his physical appearance. He believes he can help his mother return to reality by reasoning with her.

SCENE I

(Present time. The play is set in Lana's kitchen, in a suburb outside of San Francisco. The kitchen has a window and leads to the front door, which is wide open. A baking sheet full of muffins is on the counter near the table and two chairs. LANA stirs a new batch of muffin batter. She may add odd ingredients to the batter during the play, such as eggshell or thumb tacks. FRANCIS rushes in with a slight limp, holds a donut cushion in one hand and a canvas bag filled with groceries in the other. A large square of gauze is taped to his neck.)

FRANCIS: Mother?

LANA: *(She is unmoved by his presence.)* Didn't expect to see you, Frankie.

FRANCIS: Francis. Are you okay?

LANA: Is that a rhetorical question?

FRANCIS: Why is the door wide open?

LANA: Let them come. I'm ready for them.

FRANCIS: *(He closes the door.)* I know sometimes you feel frightened. But you're not alone. Everyone experiences moments when they're overwhelmed.

LANA: What the hell happened to you?

FRANCIS: Minor surgery. No big deal. *(He situates the donut cushion on the chair and sits.)*

LANA: You look like a victim in one of those vampire movies.

FRANCIS: I was hoping I would heal before our next visit. I wasn't counting on the Deputy Sheriff barging into my office, ordering me to check on my mother.

LANA: You went to work looking like that?

FRANCIS: Tell me what happened.

LANA: Nothing happened. I was defending myself. Anyway, it appears I'm in better shape than you.

FRANCIS: The cop said you nearly gave Mrs. Snodgrass a heart attack.

LANA: Sure, it's my fault.

FRANCIS: She came over to check on you—

LANA: To check on me? That woman is a meddler. Remember when the neighborhood tried to become all hoity-toity and start a neighborhood association? She made a law stating everyone's shutters had to be color-coordinated.

FRANCIS: Sure. That's ridiculous, but what do you care? Your shutters are all right.

LANA: Of course they're all right. I know what looks good. But why should some stranger who happens to live on my block decide what colors I'm allowed to paint my house? Isn't this why we live in America?

FRANCIS: For freedom of shutter-color?

LANA: Freedom of expression. The First Amendment. Not that Mrs. *Snotass* would know anything written outside of her front lawn.

FRANCIS: Some people live in small worlds, Mother. Why do you concern yourself?

LANA: I should have the right to privacy. If she keeps sticking her nose in other people's business it might get snapped off.

FRANCIS: Mother. Please. You can't make threats, even in jest.

LANA: I'm only talking to you. Even if the house is bugged, as I suspect it is, then let it stand in court where the cowards have to explain *why* they're spying on me.

FRANCIS: She came over here and then what?

LANA: She always knocks on my door and calls out my name with that voice of hers—so shrill it could shatter glass.

FRANCIS: You answered the door and?

LANA: Why would I answer the door?

FRANCIS: I don't know, Mother.

LANA: I wanted to prove that she is, in fact, a no-good, meddling spy. So I got real low. I lay just like this. *(She lies on the floor.)* Not too far from the window, but far enough where she'd have to make an effort to look in and notice my dead body.

FRANCIS: Oh Mother, you didn't.

LANA: I lay real still like this. I didn't breathe. I didn't even shut my eyes. I concentrated on my body, on what I was feeling, like in meditation class.

FRANCIS: I'm glad those classes paid off.

LANA: I concentrated on feeling the cold linoleum against my shoulders and arms. I focused my gaze on the cracks in the paint. *(Points.)* Right there. See? It looks like an upside down saxophone with a banana coming out of the end.

FRANCIS: *(He looks at the ceiling.)* Okay.

LANA: I just stared, held my breath, and waited.

FRANCIS: She looked in the window—

LANA: And screamed. You should have heard her. The funny thing is her scream is the same octave as her voice because it's so obnoxiously shrill. Though it *was* louder.

FRANCIS: And then you got up and told her you were just kidding, just conducting a social science experiment?

LANA: I waited. I wanted to see if she was genuinely concerned about my death or if she was just being dramatic for the other neighbors. Showboating witch.

FRANCIS: How can you be sure she wasn't concerned?

LANA: She's heartless. Even if she really believed I was dead, you know all that was running through her little mind was how she would tell the horrific tale to the others during one of their Neighborhood Watch brunches. My death was all about her and how she would have this great story to tell.

FRANCIS: But you're not dead.

LANA: Not yet, no. You're missing the point. This was to prove that I have no privacy.

FRANCIS: You blame her for finding you?

LANA: She shouldn't be looking in my windows. It's my business if I'm alive or dead and nobody else's.

FRANCIS: That's an interesting perspective, but mother, you can't keep acting this way. Once you start affecting the lives of others, then we enter into in a different question. If the state deems you a threat to others, then, well, you know.

LANA: I know. I know. My behavior is my choice and if I want to stay in this house … yada yada.

FRANCIS: I'm serious, mother.

LANA: You look serious, about as serious as a hit and run accident. It's sobering to see my only child in such disrepair.

FRANCIS: *(He points to his bandaged neck.)* This? You'll make fun of me, of course. Vanity over sanity every time. I had my birthmark removed. They used skin from my backside for skin grafting. More than I expected.

LANA: How could you?

FRANCIS: It was hideous. I looked like a giant gave me a hickey. Each time I met someone new, he'd stare at my neck and try to pretend he didn't really see it. It gave a bad first impression. Most people are too polite to ask about it; they just assumed I had a rowdy night or something—if only that were true.

LANA: You had no right to remove it. I made you that way.

FRANCIS: Oh please, Mother. No one plans birthmarks. No one knows why they appear. It's one of the great medical mysteries of all time.

LANA: Doctors don't know a damn thing. If they did we'd live in a much better world. You want to know where birthmarks come from? I'll tell you.

FRANCIS: Oh God.

LANA: That's right. A birthmark is a sign.

FRANCIS: Of what? God's disapproval of perfection?

LANA: My mother always told me if a child is born with a birthmark it means the mother had a wish that was unfulfilled.

FRANCIS: You're saying I'm a disappointment.

LANA: No. It usually has nothing to do with the baby. The baby is merely the product of something that happened to the mother before its birth.

FRANCIS: That's one way to put it.

LANA: I'm not talking about sex. I'm talking about life. Serious desires the mother had which never came to fruition before the pregnancy. Unless the birthmark is pink and puffy—those kinds of birthmarks come from an unfulfilled desire for strawberries.

FRANCIS: I see.

LANA: Yours was the color of burnt honey, shaped like Florida.

FRANCIS: You didn't get enough sweets and trips to Disney World?

LANA: It means I didn't live up to my purpose before I took on the responsibility of motherhood.

FRANCIS: What was your purpose?

LANA: I'll never know. But whatever it was, it didn't happen, that's for damn sure.

FRANCIS: Well, at least now the reminder of your unfulfilled wish is gone. Maybe this is a sign that you can start over and create a new purpose.

LANA: So you really did this? You surgically removed the proof of your birth. You did it for some man, right?

FRANCIS: Of course not. I never liked the way it looked. It distracted from my face. Some of my best features are up here. *(He points to his face.)* Though it's true I know the plastic surgeon quite well and he was supportive of my decision.

LANA: You and your doctors. I used to think you were a hypochondriac. Now I know better. It's not worth it. The more you change yourself for someone else, especially when it's for love, the more you lose yourself in the abyss. It's like walking along the edge of a cliff impossible to see through the fog. Later, if you survive the hike, you'll wonder where you left your soul and you'll spend the rest of your life backtracking to replace it.

FRANCIS: Let's put this stuff away. Where's Elsie?

LANA: She's long gone.

FRANCIS: What happened?

LANA: She's working with the Feds.

FRANCIS: You can't keep firing everyone. These are kind people who want to help.

LANA: I don't need any help.

FRANCIS: Everyone needs help. When you're fortunate enough to have a home, such an elegant roof over your head as this, you need people to assist with the cleaning, cooking, and—

LANA: You think I'm paranoid and yet you lie to me. Which comes first I wonder?

FRANCIS: Let's have this be a nice visit.

LANA: What's in the bag?

FRANCIS: Some groceries.

LANA: You didn't bring it, did you?

FRANCIS: What?

LANA: I wrote it in my letter. *(She gestures a gun with her hand.)*

FRANCIS: No, I didn't bring you a gun, Mother.

LANA: You'll wish you had after I'm murdered.

FRANCIS: I brought you some food.

LANA: I'm off food.

FRANCIS: How about a carton of cigarettes?

LANA: I'll take those.

FRANCIS: You've got to eat, Mother. We've been over this.

LANA: Easy for you to say. You live a reckless life.

FRANCIS: Don't start.

LANA: You and your bathhouses and imitation hamburgers.

FRANCIS: The only bathhouses are the ruins at Sutro Heights.

LANA: Ruins is right.

FRANCIS: Mother, please. I'm not the enemy here. If you didn't like Elsie, we'll find someone you do like, okay?

LANA: Always a charmer, Frankie.

FRANCIS: Francis.

LANA: Whatever.

FRANCIS: No, not whatever. My name is Francis. Frankie was my father.

LANA: That rat bastard.

FRANCIS: You named me after Saint Francis of Assisi, remember?

LANA: He was a rat bastard too.

FRANCIS: Right, he was Patron Saint of animals, particularly rat bastards.

LANA: You have no idea.

FRANCIS: Remember when you took me to New York. I was about ten and it was my first time visiting the Met.

LANA: I couldn't climb all those stairs now.

FRANCIS: And they had several paintings by El Greco. One was of Saint Francis.

LANA: They would be waiting for me inside if I did make it up the stairs.

FRANCIS: There's something mystical and deeply disturbing about his work. Each figure evokes its own light. And something in the darker shades lures you in, makes you question your perception.

LANA: They all work together, you know.

FRANCIS: El Greco took images from reality and tweaked them just enough that they became otherworldly.

LANA: At least they would be there to help me carry you out.

FRANCIS: Of course that's the only part you remember.

LANA: I thought you had died. Right there, in front of all those people. Everyone thought I was some kind of child-abuser.

FRANCIS: No one thought that.

LANA: You don't know how it is.

FRANCIS: Your son passes out in front of "Saint Francis of Assisi in Prayer," *(He poses like Francis in the painting: right hand over his heart, the left outstretched with ballet fingers, head downward and humble.)* and you worry what people think of you? Christ!

LANA: Don't blaspheme.

FRANCIS: You just called Saint Francis a rat bastard.

LANA: So what? I'm your mother.

FRANCIS: It's really good to see you.

LANA: You should visit more often.

FRANCIS: I know.

LANA: He really did look like you, even more now that you're grown.

FRANCIS: Well, I may bear a *slight* resemblance to the figure in the painting. If you can't live like a saint, you might as well look like one.

LANA: I still don't understand why they did that.

FRANCIS: No one did anything. I fainted from sheer excitement.

LANA: Happens all the time, does it?

FRANCIS: That's why I never leave home without my smelling salts.

LANA: Is that what they're calling it these days?

FRANCIS: I see you've made some muffins.

(FRANCIS picks up a muffin. Before he can take a bite, LANA lunges at him and snatches it from his hand.)

LANA: No! Don't eat it!

FRANCIS: Why not?

LANA: They're not for you.

FRANCIS: Really.

LANA: I made them with rat poison. I leave them here on the counter, you see. If they don't get the intruders, at least they kill the rats.

FRANCIS: Mother! You could kill someone.

LANA: That's the idea. Self-defense.

FRANCIS: This is really dangerous. I wish I didn't know. This is the kind of act that could get you in real trouble. You could be sent away for life. And now I could be an accessory.

LANA: I'm not passing these out on the street. I'm not inviting people over and serving them poisonous food. The muffins stay here on the counter. Think of this as a creative mousetrap. In the privacy—or so-called privacy—of my home I make something that belongs to me. If someone comes into my house, uninvited, and eats one of my muffins and dies, it's not my problem. No one should be in my home without asking. It's the same thing as shooting an intruder in self-defense. Now, if you would just bring a gun like I asked for I wouldn't have to bake with rat poison.

FRANCIS: So it's my fault.

LANA: Well, I don't like to put it that way.

FRANCIS: What's with this fixation on guns? When I was a kid you wouldn't even let me play with a water gun.

LANA: I'm not safe here.

FRANCIS: I'm sorry you feel that way. Maybe I should hire some bodyguards.

LANA: Nice try.

FRANCIS: I need you to promise me you won't do this anymore.

LANA: Don't pretend you care.

FRANCIS: It's never enough. No matter how hard I try, I'm always disappointing you.

LANA: Well, you could try a little harder.

FRANCIS: Doing what?

LANA: You don't visit very often.

FRANCIS: I'm here now.

LANA: Because the Sheriff made you.

FRANCIS: Oh come on.

LANA: Everyone wants something. No one does anything unless they can get something out of it for themselves.

FRANCIS: What about you, Mother? What do you want?

LANA: I want these damn vultures to stop following me. Hovering over me, waiting for their chance to pounce, to gobble up my flesh before I've even hit the ground.

FRANCIS: Who are these vultures?

LANA: You haven't even been here fifteen minutes and you're calling me crazy.

FRANCIS: I never use the "C" word, Mother.

LANA: They're always watching me. It's as if I were on stage before a live audience every heartbreaking moment of my life.

FRANCIS: No one's watching you.

LANA: That's what they want you to believe.

FRANCIS: Okay. Who's watching you? Give examples. And I don't want to hear anymore about Mrs. Snodgrass.

LANA: Did you see that box in front of the house?

FRANCIS: *(He looks out the window.)* I don't see any box.

LANA: The box on the pole in front of my house. It's been there since Frankie bought the place before you were born.

FRANCIS: The mailbox?

LANA: I refuse to call it that anymore.

FRANCIS: Too much junk mail?

LANA: Every day a man in a blue uniform—

FRANCIS: The mailman.

LANA: *Dressed* like the mailman. He spends about twenty minutes out there trying to stuff papers in the box. Eventually he yanks all of them out and walks up the path to my door, pretending to deliver the mail.

FRANCIS: And do you answer the door?

LANA: Are you crazy? I watch him as he goes. Sometimes he takes the bundle of papers with him to his truck. Other times he rolls them up and jams them into the box so they hang halfway out and eventually fall into the street. He reports to the others as soon as he gets in the truck. They're waiting in the back, where I can't see their faces, but I see him looking in the rearview mirror, reporting how yet again I've slipped through their nefarious fingers.

FRANCIS: Okay. So, hypothetically, if your story were accurate, when does the real mailman deliver the mail?

LANA: You receive all of my bills. So there shouldn't be any mail coming here.

FRANCIS: That's not how it works.

LANA: Who could possibly be sending mail to me?

FRANCIS: Companies who want to sell their products.

LANA: How do they get my address? I'm very careful about giving out my personal information.

FRANCIS: Well … Why are they watching you?

LANA: They want me dead.

FRANCIS: That seems awfully drastic.

LANA: Not really. You see, I'm a threat to them.

FRANCIS: *(Exasperated.)* Mother, please. I don't know how to get through to you. I keep hoping you'll finally snap out of it and come back to me. There was a time when you were, well, more relaxed.

LANA: I don't use drugs.

FRANCIS: I think there's a lot to be said for today's psychopharmaceuticals.

LANA: Stale!

FRANCIS: What?

LANA: We've been down this manhole. It's a stale argument.

FRANCIS: I know there was one prescription that didn't agree with you, but—

LANA: Didn't agree? It nearly killed me! And it nearly killed Father Moore.

FRANCIS: I still don't understand what you and Father Moore were doing in a Mahjong parlor.

LANA: Parlor makes it sound seedy. It was a Chinatown casino.

FRANCIS: And?

LANA: We were invited there by a family—

FRANCIS: *(Mocking.) The* family?

LANA: Don't be paranoid. Why would they want anything to do with a priest and an abandoned housewife? Father Moore makes a point of visiting every gaming establishment west of the Mississippi.

FRANCIS: Get them while they're having fun.

LANA: He's such a good man. He doesn't use his divine connection while he's gambling. That's for sure. Poor thing owes money all over. He plays fair. If I were a priest I'd move to Vegas, cash in on my calling. Of course I'd donate some of my winnings to the church.

FRANCIS: Why did he bring you along?

LANA: For my muffins.

FRANCIS: Excuse me? How long have you been putting poison in your muffins?

LANA: Oh no. I didn't start doing that until recently. This was way back, around the time Frankie left. I didn't know what to do. I was suddenly a single mother who had wasted the best years of my life on a man who never loved me. There I was: middle-aged and entirely spent. There was no point in going on.

FRANCIS: I was in the picture, wasn't I?

LANA: Right, of course. And you were a handful, with your fainting spells and obsession with art. You couldn't just paint pictures of inanimate fruits and veggies. No, you had to sneak out and paint the town—literally.

FRANCIS: Graffiti is a valid art form.

LANA: It's not for perfectionists. It's all about timing and placement. You kept getting arrested because you'd insist on standing there hours after the sun came up, determined to get the picture absolutely the way you imagined it, which any artist will tell you is impossible. With your free hand you continued painting even as the cops handcuffed the other.

FRANCIS: Back then I believed I was some sort of visionary, that my work might actually mean something.

LANA: Growing up's a drag, isn't it?

FRANCIS: I used to resent you for being so supportive. You always told me I could be whatever I wanted to be and I believed you. When I realized that was just a legend, a well-meaning lie people tell their kids to buy into, like Santa Claus, I was way too old to kick and scream and be sent to my room.

LANA: People should raise their kids with realistic expectations. They should tell them to have fun while they're young because with every moment of age comes the weight of bad circumstances and regret. Eventually it becomes so heavy it suffocates you like being steam-rolled under wet cement.

FRANCIS: Jesus.

LANA: Don't blaspheme.

FRANCIS: By taking you to Chinatown Father Moore helped you realize you were not being steam-rolled by life?

LANA: After Frankie left I thought about killing myself. And there was that one episode when I ate your paints.

FRANCIS: I have never been able to replace "Azure Fields."

LANA: Those damn environmental laws. When I was a kid paints were made with lead and were highly toxic.

FRANCIS: Ah, the good old days. I can just taste the DDT on my apple.

LANA: After I ate your paints and suffered mild indigestion and the rather colorful exodus from my system, I feared I would be sent to hell. So I called Father Moore and asked him to read my Last Rites.

FRANCIS: You weren't dying.

LANA: But I was. Emotionally. People die every moment from heartbreak, which is exactly what I told Father Moore.

FRANCIS: He didn't read your Last Rites.

LANA: No. But he helped me realize why I'm here and how I'm part of God's plan.

FRANCIS: To make muffins?

LANA: That's only part of the plan. You see, Frankie had stolen my identity. Over the course of our marriage he made me change in so many ways. He made me quit smoking, dye my hair, vote. My interests became his. I didn't know what I liked to eat, what I thought about current events. I only knew what *he* thought. I pretended to believe things I didn't really believe all those years, without even knowing it. When he left and wasn't here to continue chipping away at my identity, I realized I had become a stranger to myself.

FRANCIS: Father Moore kindly stepped in and gave you a new set of beliefs to buy into.

LANA: He helped me try to remember who I was before I fell in love with Frankie.

FRANCIS: Who were you?

LANA: Betty Crocker, but drop dead gorgeous. Father Moore used to say, "Focus on the positive." My earliest positive memory was baking. I remember looking up at my mother as she baked. She used to wear this awful egg shell-colored apron. It used to be white I suppose. I grew so used to seeing her in that apron I even argued to have her buried in it. She was radiant as she stood over the stove, stirring, making new concoctions. The possibilities were endless. With each recipe I imagined presenting my work to a suitor who is so moved he would propose marriage right there on the spot.

FRANCIS: It's good you had realistic expectations.

LANA: Father Moore told me to remember this each time I think about ending my life. I replace those thoughts with the smell of fresh cinnamon rolls.

FRANCIS: So you found happiness through baking.

LANA: It calms me. Back then I was still completing my state-required visits with Dr. Bluntmeyer. He's the one that prescribed those awful pills.

FRANCIS: Some of his prescriptions worked.

LANA: No. None of them worked. Thorzine made me jittery. It was impossible to stand still. I was always in motion. I was like a shark, constantly moving forward, with dead eyes and an insatiable desire that could only be fed by destruction. When I told the doctor he changed my prescription to some generic form of Haldol that was eventually yanked from the market.

FRANCIS: But they have new drugs now. They're improving them day-by-day.

LANA: Aha! If they were good they wouldn't need to be improved.

FRANCIS: That's not how it works and you know it. That something serves its function is never enough. There's always a market for more. Look at toothbrushes. Every drugstore has at least three rows of toothbrushes. Packaging boasts of new angles that will surely remove all bacteria and plaque like never before. Find colors and name brands to match your favorite cavity-fighting toothpaste. And those are just the regular toothbrushes we haven't even gotten to the electric ones.

LANA: Are you still dating that dentist?

FRANCIS: No. I've met someone new.

LANA: I don't want to hear about it. I'll just get my hopes up again.

FRANCIS: *Your* hopes?

LANA: A mother wants only the best for her son.

FRANCIS: If you wanted the best for me—

LANA: Can't say it anymore, can you? It's so stale. If we say the same things enough times they eventually lose their meaning. Even if we continue saying the words after we've forgotten their meaning the instinct that drove us to say them is also forgotten. Repetition is like gangrene.

FRANCIS: There are moments like right now when I imagine everything, all those embarrassing slips like when you showed up at my glass blowing class in the nude, I almost let myself believe those memories are unreal, that they're *my* delusions and that you're actually the wisest person that ever was and could never be a victim of mental illness.

LANA: I'm no victim.

FRANCIS: I didn't mean victim, I meant—

LANA: It was too hot in the glass blowing studio. I did nothing wrong. You see, they want me to be a victim. They want me dead.

FRANCIS: All right, all right. Finish talking about Father Moore.

LANA: He invited me to go with him to the Mahjong parlor. I baked two batches of muffins to thank the family for including us. Even before we got there I had the sense that we were being watched. Someone was following us. Father Moore didn't agree and I gradually understood that he was in on it. As he played Mahjong with the others I stood in the back with my muffins, which were untouched. Everyone was eating a cake that the host's wife prepared. You see, to partake in the joy of my muffins would make them feel guilty after they killed me. Father Moore was winning. They must be letting him win, I thought.

FRANCIS: Why would they let him win?

LANA: It was part of their plan to bring my guard down so they could sneak up behind me and slash my throat.

FRANCIS: Jesus.

LANA: Don't blaspheme. It was those new pills. Dr. Bluntmeyer had just changed my prescription. This was the first day on the new drug. Instead of the shakes the pills made me see a little too clearly.

FRANCIS: You still don't believe you were suffering paranoid delusions that day?

LANA: I said what I needed to say to get out of that prison. It's a matter of survival. I did my time. You put too much stock in psychology speak. All they do is invent language to describe things that can't really be pinned down by words. Life is far too complicated for their silly categories. Maybe if you'd realize that you'd stop having so many affairs with doctors.

FRANCIS: Affairs are noncommittal flings, Mother. I engage in *relationships* so passionate and strong that they're simply unsustainable.

LANA: After two rounds of the game I realized what I had to do. I wouldn't give them the satisfaction of killing me. I wanted them to know I was aware of their plan. I would kill Father Moore first and then myself. I grabbed the cake knife and charged at him. But all I managed to do was stain Father Moore's collar with chocolate icing.

FRANCIS: Do you remember the time you spent in the hospital?

LANA: That place was a prison.

FRANCIS: Father Moore visited you there. Do you remember?

LANA: I remember he testified against me and said it was God's will that I stay in that awful place.

FRANCIS: And did you believe him?

LANA: Of course I did. It's all part of the plan.

FRANCIS: Then wouldn't it also be part of the plan for you to take your prescribed medicine?

LANA: Is that why you're here? You want to drug me all the time. Just like your father. You want to steal my identity.

FRANCIS: Mother. I don't want you to be sent away again. But I need your help. The neighbors keep calling the cops. You fire the people hired to assist you. Now there are poisoned muffins involved. If you threaten any more people they'll send you away. And you've seen the state facility. Rooms crowded with drooling people who look as though they've been struck by lightning, splotchy gray walls that reek of bleach and urine, weeds growing out of the corner of the floor. The private institution isn't much better. But to send you there I'll have to sell your house to make the payments. Is that what you want?

LANA: You're in on it.

FRANCIS: Answer me. Is that what you want?

LANA: I don't care anymore. I know I'm marked for death and I don't even care. I just want them to hurry up and get on with it.

FRANCIS: *(He pulls out a prescription bottle from the bag and tries to hand it to her.)* Please.

LANA: You think an orange bottle of pills will make it all go away?

FRANCIS: Well, it would certainly make *me* feel better.

LANA: Where did you get those?

FRANCIS: A close friend of mine is a psychiatrist. He's agreed to meet with you, and if you like him, he'll add you to his client list.

LANA: I'm through with doctors.

FRANCIS: Mother, the Sheriff gave me an ultimatum. He said if you don't accept responsibility and start seeing a professional again, then he'll have to take action. You know what that means. That means you lose your house. It means you really won't have privacy or choices.

LANA: The government is always trying to run my life.

FRANCIS: It's your choice. Right now you still have the freedom to decide. I believe you can get better. But you have to *want* to get better.

LANA: Why would the government grant me such an important decision if I'm so crazy?

FRANCIS: That's a good question, Mother. All I know is this may be your last chance, your last opportunity to make a decision. Will you please try?

LANA: *(She accepts the bottle of pills reluctantly.)* Will you visit me tomorrow?

FRANCIS: If you start taking your medicine I'll visit you every three days. How about that?

(LANA pops a pill into her mouth.)

FRANCIS: Thank you, Mother. This really means a lot to me. I know life can be overwhelming at times. It's important to remember we're all in this together. Each and every one of us lives in an absurd world. How we choose to cope with it is what makes us individuals.

LANA: I understand now.

FRANCIS: I knew you would. I never gave up hope.

LANA: It's a matter of survival.

FRANCIS: That's right. I can't tell you how happy you've made me.

(FRANCIS tosses the tray of poisoned muffins into the trashcan.)

LANA: What are you doing?

FRANCIS: *(He takes the trash bag to the door.)* Now that we're starting a new beginning we don't want to accidentally poison anyone, do we? I'll be right back.

(FRANCIS exits with the trash. LANA pours the bottle of pills into the batter, and stirs them in.)

(Blackout)
(The End)

*Armin Parsanejad as NICK, Chiara Montalto as DANNI
and Jennie West (Standing) as GRACE in ALWAYS, ANASTASIA in
The Riant Theatre's Strawberry One-Act Festival Winter 2008
at The American Theater of Actors in NYC*

ALWAYS, ANASTASIA
By Michele Leigh

Michele Leigh is a graduate of Western Connecticut State University (WCSU), where she earned an Associates of Science in Liberal Arts. In 2007, her *Psychobiography of Marilyn Monroe* was published in the WCSU Honors Journal. Michele is a member of the Writer's Guild of America and the Dramatist Guild.

Always, Anastasia was first produced in the Riant Theater's 2008 Strawberry Festival. It was selected to participate in the Wild Night series with the following cast:

NICK	Armin Parsanejad
DANNI	Chiara Montalto
GRACE	Jennie West

This play was directed by Michele Leigh.

CAST OF CHARACTERS:

NICK, A disillusioned cop in his mid-thirties. Nick fulfilled his childhood dream of becoming a NYC police officer but feels disappointed by the reality of it. Nick's only family is his wife Grace, whom he adores. He is a recovering alcoholic who has been sober for nine years. He is obsessive-compulsive, paranoid and has difficulty sleeping.
DANNI, Nick's partner in her mid-twenties. Danni is an over-achiever who is a good cop, but always feels the need to prove herself. She is optimistic, ambitious and eager to learn from Nick's experience. She is a tom-boy (yet still feminine) who is likable to both men and women.
GRACE, Nick's wife, a vocalist in her mid-thirties. Grace began singing at an early age and throughout her life used music as a means of escaping the world around her. She is extremely talented but not at all ambitious. She sings with a

local chamber choir but prefers to spend time at home with her husband, Nick and their cat, Felix.

SCENE I

(Lights up. It is a cold evening at the end of February. NICK is alone in his apartment sitting on the couch. He is wearing his gun and badge. He looks weary and in need of a shave. He pulls a bottle of Absolute vodka from under the coffee table. He places the bottle on top of the coffee table and stares at it. The TV is playing the local news. The TV is assumed and the audience only hears the audio.)

TV: And we are back with an official plea from local authorities to help locate the notorious Anastasia, who recently escaped from Willow Pines Psychiatric Prison. Anastasia shocked the authorities on December, 8th when she disappeared during a routine hospital transfer. Anastasia served more than twelve years of a life sentence when she confessed to killing her three small children, by strapping them in their car seats, and rolling the car into the Hudson River.

(Doorbell.)

TV: As the search continues, the hotlines are burning up with alleged sightings of Anastasia, but the police are still unable to locate the fugitive.

(Doorbell.)

TV: If you have seen this woman or know of her whereabouts, you are urged to call 1-800-312-6038.

(Doorbell.)

NICK: *(Quickly hides bottle and heads for door.)* I'm coming. I'm coming.

TV: In other news tonight …

(NICK opens front door and DANNI enters holding a bundle of mail.)

DANNI: Hey Nick, how's it going? Wow, you look like shit!

NICK: *(Sarcastically.)* Thanks. It's nice to see you too, Danni.

DANNI: When's the last time you slept man?

NICK: I dunno. I don't sleep good these days.

DANNI: I just thought I'd come by and check up on you. Here, I picked up your mail. It was piling up down there.

NICK: Thanks, throw it anywhere. I just made a pot of coffee. You want a cup? *(NICK exits to kitchen, off-stage left.)*

DANNI: Yeah, sure. *(Dropping mail on coffee table and removing her coat to reveal gun and badge.)* Hey, it's the middle of February. Might be time to take down that Christmas tree, don't you think?

NICK: *(Calling from kitchen.)* I believe "they" say you officially have till the last day of winter to take down your tree.

DANNI: Oh really? Just what the hell do "they" know anyway?

NICK: *(Enters from kitchen holding two cups of coffee. Hands one to DANNI and plops on couch.)* Look ... Me and Grace decorated that tree together on Christmas Eve. I refuse to take it down until my wife is home safe and sound. You can understand that right?

DANNI: Still no sign of her, huh?

NICK: Nope. Last time I saw her was Christmas Eve. What's the word down at the station?

DANNI: Well, her credit cards and bank cards haven't been used since December 24th. Her cell phone either.

NICK: *(Impatiently.)* Yeah, yeah I know all that! What about the DNA from the hairbrush I gave you?

DANNI: We ran Grace's DNA through the main database and came up with zilch.

NICK: I can't believe that the entire NYPD can't find my wife! This is total bullshit!

DANNI: We're doing all we can Nick. You know the drill. Aren't you a part of the NYPD?

NICK: Well right now, I'm not! I've been suspended for that bullshit anonymous complaint!

DANNI: The suspension is just a formality until the complaint can be investigated. Besides you are in no condition to go back to work. Let's take a reality check here.

NICK: Oh yeah? How's this for a reality check? Most mornings I wake up in the pit of hell and I have never needed a drink so badly in my entire life!

DANNI: You've been sober for what? Nine years now?

NICK: Nine years, seven months, and four days. But the little voice telling you to drink never really goes away you know? That's just some bullshit line they feed you.

DANNI: Sounds like you need to get your ass to a meeting.

NICK: Spare me the lecture.

DANNI: Hey, they warned us about this shit in the Academy, you know?

NICK: Ah yes, the Academy. What was that? Like two years ago for you?

DANNI: Five years! Thank you very much.

NICK: Man, five years out of the academy. I remember what that was like.

DANNI: What was it like for you?

NICK: It was a time of optimism. A time where I thought I could do anything. Thought I could take on the world. But you know what they say, no matter how invincible you perceive yourself to be ... You. Are. Wrong.

DANNI: So how about now? After fifteen years on the force?

NICK: Hmmm let's see. Well, the ten-year-countdown to pension begins. And this is usually the time when a cop officially crosses the line from bitter to jaded.

DANNI: Oh yeah? And just when does a cop become bitter?

NICK: Well, that all depends.

DANNI: When did you become bitter?

NICK: I can't really remember anymore.

DANNI: Can't remember? Or don't want to remember?

NICK: *(Getting annoyed.)* Why don't you call me in ten years and let me know how you feel then? After you've seen half the shit I've seen. When I worked the Anastasia case, I realized that people are capable of absolutely anything.

DANNI: I was wondering how long it would take for Anastasia to work her way into the conversation.

NICK: Well, I was just watching the news and they were running another story on her. What is the world's fascination with that crazy bitch?

DANNI: The world's fascination? Or your fascination?

NICK: Come on, I'm allowed to obsess a little bit.

DANNI: True, you were the arresting officer, but lots of cops worked that case.

NICK: Yeah, but I spent a lot of time with her and she always seemed to fixate on me. Man, she was one scary bitch let me tell you.

DANNI: Come on. She's a child killer, not a cop killer.

NICK: I'm not saying she's gonna kill me. I'm just saying that she's fucking with my head.

DANNI: What do you mean?

NICK: Well ever since she escaped from the nuthouse, she's been sending me these letters.

DANNI: What kind of letters?

NICK: Cryptic letters. Letters that arrive in pale blue envelopes. She must be hand delivering them for Christ's sake! I feel like she's watching me.

DANNI: Wow, you really are paranoid.

NICK: Paranoid huh? You sound just like Grace on Christmas Eve ...

(NICK looks over at Christmas tree and DANNI follows his gaze. They both freeze as the lights go down. Christmas tree becomes illuminated.)

GRACE: *(Singing in front of Christmas tree.)* Silent night, holy night, All is calm, all is bright, Round yon Virgin Mother and Child, Holy Infant so tender and mild, Sleep in heavenly peace, Sleep in heavenly peace.

SCENE II

(Lights up. GRACE turns to tree and begins decorating with NICK. They are sipping egg nog and enjoying Christmas Eve in a flashback.)

GRACE: *(Holding an ornament in the air.)* Oh look, this ornament was for Felix. Man I miss that cat.

NICK: It's unbelievable how much I miss the little guy.

GRACE: Sometimes, out of the corner of my eye, I still think I see him running around.

NICK: Hey did we ever get that report back from the vet?

GRACE: Oh yeah, I think I saw something in the mail today. *(Flipping through mail on end table.)* Yes, here it is.

NICK: *(Opening report and reading.)* OK … let's see … Felix … feline … yeah, yeah … here we go … cause of death … *(Pause.)* … toxic substance found in digestive system.

GRACE: Toxic substance?

NICK: Probable poisoning.

GRACE: Poison?

NICK: That bitch!

GRACE: What bitch?

NICK: Anastasia!

GRACE: Oh my God. Again with Anastasia. You are obsessed with that woman!

NICK: You saw that letter! She killed Felix! I just know it. That's what she threatened to do!

GRACE: Wait a minute. When did Anastasia threaten to kill Felix?

NICK: Don't you remember? She said that we would lose the thing that gives us comfort or something. Where is that frigging letter?

(NICK exits to bedroom, off-stage right.)

GRACE: You think, Anastasia came in here and poisoned our cat? How would she get into the apartment?

NICK: *(Calling from bedroom.)* Anything is possible. Don't be so naïve!

GRACE: Oh, I'm being naïve? I think your being paranoid!

NICK: *(Returning from bedroom with letter.)* Here it is. Read it. Go ahead, read it!

GRACE: Dear Nick. May each of your creature comforts slowly disappear. Always, Anastasia.

NICK: Felix was a creature! Felix was a comfort! I can't believe that bitch killed our cat!

GRACE: Calm down. Let's not talk about her again tonight. Come on, its Christmas Eve. Hey, instead of waiting for midnight, let's each open one gift now. I bet that would change the vibe in here.

(GRACE retrieves a gift from kitchen and NICK retrieves a gift from bedroom. They meet on the couch and open gifts at the same time.)

GRACE: Oh wow! It's that Christmas tree topper we saw up in Quebec City!

NICK: Yup. I went back to the store and bought it that night after you fell asleep. Oh hey, a wallet, thanks!

GRACE: *(Still admiring the tree topper.)* It's beautiful; I love it, thank you! Let's put it on the tree.

(GRACE hands the tree topper to NICK as the phone rings.)

GRACE: *(Answering phone.)* Hello ... Oh hey Ginny ... no way ... not tonight! ... what time? ... till when? ... But, it's Christmas eve ... I know ... all right ... I'll see you in a bit ... bye. *(Hanging up phone.)* Ginny says that Malcolm is freaking out about the show tomorrow. He wants to run through the Mendelssohn piece one more time.

NICK: Are you kidding me?

GRACE: *(Exiting to bedroom, off-stage right.)* I am so sorry. I should be back by 10:00. It's still Christmas Eve till midnight. Will you wait up for me?

NICK: Well, that all depends.

GRACE: *(Appearing in doorway with coat on.)* I'll make it worth your while.

NICK: *(Laughing.)* Yeah, yeah, I'll see you later.

GRACE: *(Exiting through front door.)* Love you, Ciao!

(Lights down. Christmas tree lights off.)

SCENE III

(Lights up. Back to the present. NICK and DANNI are still seated on the couch finishing their coffee.)

NICK: When she wasn't back by 10:00, I started calling around. Nobody had heard from her. By midnight, I was frantic.

DANNI: So, Grace never even made it to the rehearsal?

NICK: Nope. She was probably waiting for her down in the parking garage?

DANNI: Who was waiting for her?

NICK: Anastasia.

DANNI: Wait a minute. You think Anastasia had something to do with Grace's disappearance?

NICK: I wouldn't put it past her. She killed my cat and then ... wait a minute, she warned me about this. *(Frantically looking around.)* Where the hell is it?

DANNI: What are you looking for?

NICK: Another letter from Anastasia, I got it right before Grace disappeared. *(Pulling a letter from under the coffee table.)* Here it is. Here it is. Dear Nick. May the person you love begin to fill you with fear. Always Anastasia. See?

DANNI: First of all, we can't be sure that Anastasia is actually sending these letters. There's no return address and no stamp. Secondly, where does it say she's gonna kidnap Grace?

NICK: Grace is the one I love! Don't you get it? She's threatening me!

DANNI: These letters are not really threats, Nick. They're more like … like fucked up fortune cookies. Look, this is not purely a social call.

NICK: Never is.

DANNI: It's about that anonymous complaint.

NICK: I told you already. I had nothing to do with that assault and battery charge.

DANNI: Yeah, well someone assaulted and battered that guy pretty bad. And he's convinced it was you.

NICK: Why would I beat up a total stranger?

DANNI: Claims you were drunk off your ass at the time. Plus he knows some people in high places and he's been making some noise and …

NICK: And what?

DANNI: And your gonna need to turn in your gun and badge until this whole thing is sorted out.

NICK: Oh, this is complete bullshit!

DANNI: It's just a formality until the complaint can be investigated and cleared.

NICK: *(Ignoring her request and flipping through mail on coffee table.)* Holy Crap! I got another one!

DANNI: Another what?

NICK: Another letter from Anastasia.

DANNI: You've gotta be kidding me?

NICK: *(Waving envelope at DANNI.)* It was in the pile of mail you brought up with you. Look a pale blue envelope and no stamp!

DANNI: I doubt she delivered it herself. Someone might have recognized her. *(Taking letter from NICK and reading.)* Dear Nick. May you lose the skills you need to survive. Always, Anastasia.

(NICK silently removes his gun and badge and grudgingly hands them to DANNI. Lights down.)

SCENE IV

(Lights up. It is about a month later, the last day of winter. NICK is alone in his apartment, sleeping on the couch and fully clothed. The apartment is a mess. The TV is assumed and the audience only hears the audio.)

TV: Good afternoon today is Tuesday, March 20ᵗʰ and it is officially the last day of winter. There has been a new development in the investigation of an unidentified female body retrieved from the Hudson River early Sunday morning.

(Doorbell.)

TV: Although the body was badly deteriorated, the medical examiner was able to determine that the woman was thirteen weeks pregnant at the time of her death.

(Doorbell.)

NICK: *(Jumping awake with panic and heading for door.)* Yeah, yeah, hang on.

TV: Circumstances surrounding her death are still unknown.

(NICK opens front door and DANNI enters.)

DANNI: *(Looking him up and down.)* Hey Nick, how are you doing?

NICK: *(Shrugging.)* Same shit, different day. Any news on Grace?

DANNI: Not exactly, but check this out. There was a woman who showed up in Philly with no recollection of her past. She seemed to match Grace's description so ...

NICK: So? What?

DANNI: We sent down Grace's DNA, but it wasn't a match.

NICK: Damn it! Something like that would have made sense you know? Like maybe she just slipped on the ice, hit her head and got amnesia. That kind of thing happens all the time, right? *(Trailing off.)* Yeah, yeah ... that's what happened, she got amnesia ...

DANNI: Hey, are you OK?

NICK: *(Avoiding eye contact.)* What? Yeah, sure, sure. I just couldn't sleep last night.

DANNI: Anyway, we've been testing Grace's DNA with every Jane Doe that passes through the city morgue. We still haven't hit a match, so that's somewhat encouraging.

NICK: *(Sarcastically.)* Oh yeah ... there's the silver lining.

DANNI: It's ridiculous how long it takes to run DNA tests.

NICK: Tell me about it.

DANNI: They put a DNA rush on the body they pulled out of the Hudson River. But even with all the media attention, the results don't seem to come back any faster.

NICK: Oh yeah, they were talking about that floater on the news.

DANNI: Hey, do you think it could be? Oh never mind.

NICK: What?

DANNI: Do you think it could be Anastasia's body?

NICK: Anastasia's body? Huh! That would be nice.

DANNI: Nice? Do you really think that you'd feel better if Anastasia were dead?

NICK: Not sure if better is the right word, but I sure would feel relieved.

DANNI: *(Changing the subject.)* Hey, can I bug you for a cup of coffee?

NICK: Sure, why not?

(NICK exits to kitchen, off-stage left.)

DANNI: Thanks.

(As soon as NICK exits, DANNI pulls a black light and a bottle of luminal from her coat pockets. Quickly looking around she sprays the coffee table and illuminates the black light across the surface. No blood is detected.)

NICK: *(Calling from kitchen.)* Jesus Christ, This woman will not give up!

DANNI: *(Distracted.)* What's that?

NICK: *(Calling from kitchen.)* I just found another letter from Anastasia!

DANNI: *(Still distracted.)* Oh yeah?

NICK: Listen to this. Dear Nick. May you become the very thing you despise. Always Anastasia. What the fuck is that supposed to mean?

(DANNI sprays the couch and illuminates the black light across the surface. No blood is detected. NICK suddenly enters from kitchen.)

NICK: And what the fuck is going on in here!?

DANNI: Don't freak out. Let me explain.

NICK: You better explain what the hell your doing in my apartment with a black light and a bottle of luminal!

DANNI: Look, they've been talking down at the station.

NICK: Oh really? And exactly what have they been saying down at the station?

DANNI: They've been saying that the body pulled from the Hudson River might be Grace.

NICK: My Grace?

DANNI: And you and I both know that when a wife shows up dead, the prime suspect is always the husband.

NICK: Is there something you'd like to ask me Danni?

DANNI: Did you have anything to do with Grace's disappearance?

NICK: No.

DANNI: Are you drinking again?

NICK: What is this? An interrogation?

DANNI: Look, I want to believe you.

NICK: You think I'm drinking again? You think I'm getting into barroom brawls with strangers and drowning my wife in the Hudson River? Is that what you really think of me?

DANNI: Look, if Grace's DNA is a match, I'm gonna need to eliminate you as a suspect.

NICK: Then do your research Detective!

DANNI: What do you mean?

NICK: The woman they found in the river was pregnant, right?

DANNI: Yeah, so?

NICK: Grace and I couldn't have kids.

DANNI: I didn't know that.

NICK: Just get the hell out of here.

(DANNI exits through front door. NICK plops down on couch with black light and spray bottle. He grabs the Anastasia letters from under the coffee table along with the bottle of vodka. He quickly twists off the cap and drinks directly from the bottle. He reads each of the four letters aloud and continues to drink.)

NICK: Dear Nick. May each of your creature comforts slowly disappear. May the person you love begin to fill you with fear. May you lose all the skills you need to survive. May you become the very thing you despise. Always, Anastasia.

(NICK gets up and starts pacing in front of the Christmas tree. He is holding the black light and spray bottle.)

NICK: Husbands are usually the most likely suspects. Little Miss know-it-all. Are you drinking again? Nosey bitch! Who the hell does she think she is?

(NICK stops pacing and stares at the Christmas tree. He slowly and deliberately sprays the Christmas tree with luminal. He waves the black light up the tree. Blood splatters become visible. When he gets to the tree topper, the black light reveals a bloody hand print. NICK freezes. Lights down. Black light off. The Christmas tree becomes illuminated.)

GRACE: *(Singing in front of Christmas tree.)* Silent night, holy night! Shepherds quake at the sight. Glories stream from heaven afar. Heavenly hosts sing Alleluia! Christ, the Savior is born. Christ, the Savior is born.

SCENE V

(Lights up. GRACE turns to tree and begins decorating with NICK. They are sipping eggnog and trying to enjoy Christmas Eve in a flashback. There is a quiet tension between them which escalates into full blown rage.)

GRACE: *(Holding up an ornament.)* Oh look, this ornament was for Felix. Man, I miss that little guy.

NICK: Yeah, me too.

GRACE: What do you mean, you too? You're the one who killed him.

NICK: I did not kill Felix.

GRACE: The vet's report said he was poisoned by a toxic substance.

NICK: I told you already, I didn't know that Poinsettia plants were toxic to cats.

GRACE: Well, maybe you would have been more aware if you weren't half loaded all the time.

NICK: Here we go. Are you going to get on my case about the drinking again?

GRACE: So you admit that you are drinking again?

NICK: Yeah, but I can handle it! Everything in moderation Gracie. Speaking of which, how about we spice up these eggnogs with a little Christmas cheer?

(NICK adds vodka to his eggnog glass.)

GRACE: Have you forgotten how bad it gets when you drink, Nick? You were sober for nine years. I can't believe that you're just gonna throw that all away?

NICK: Look, I'm under a lot of pressure OK?

GRACE: And drinking helps you deal with the pressure?

NICK: I can't believe your gonna bust my balls when I have this Anastasia shit to deal with. Do you realize that crazy bitch is out there roaming the streets!

GRACE: Oh, it's Anastasia's fault now? It's always someone else's fault. Anastasia is just sending you strange little letters. You're the one turning them into self-fulfilling prophecies.

NICK: But, Anastasia is the one who sent the Poinsettia plant! She knew the plant would kill our cat!

GRACE: You have such a vivid imagination. The card that came with the plant was simply blank. The florist must have screwed up. Why do you always think that everyone is out to get you?

NICK: Not everyone. Just Anastasia. First she sends the poisonous plant that kills Felix, then she files the phony complaint that gets me suspended, and then …

GRACE: You and I both know who filed that complaint.

NICK: Oh, that's right. You think it was that punk in the restaurant who was trying to get into your pants, right?

GRACE: Oh yeah, he was trying to get into my pants you idiot! He just opened the door for me! You're the maniac who started pummeling him!

NICK: Please Grace; he opened the door so he could get a better look at your ass!

GRACE: Oh, that' right, another side effect of your drinking is insane jealousy.

NICK: I'm not a fool Grace. You and Anastasia, you both think I'm a fool, but I'm not. I'm a cop you know? I get paid to be observant.

GRACE: *(Under her breath.)* Yeah, you're Mr. Observant all right.

(NICK refills his glass with vodka. He offers it to GRACE, but she shakes her head and sits on the couch.)

NICK: Let's take a look at the cold hard facts here, shall we? You "work late" almost every night. When you are here, you're completely preoccupied. And you never want to have sex anymore. Oh, and let's not forget the late night phone calls with you whispering into the phone to God-knows-who?

GRACE: I'm not going to play this game tonight. *(Pause.)* Hey, instead of waiting for midnight, let's each open one gift now. I bet that would change the vibe in here.

NICK: Yeah, sure.

(GRACE exits to kitchen, off stage left.)

NICK: *(Raising his glass in a mock toast and exiting to bedroom, off-stage right.)* Merry freaking Christmas!

(Phone rings.)

GRACE: *(Entering from kitchen with gift and answering phone.)* Hello ... Oh hey Ginny ... no way ... not tonight! ... what time? ... till when? ... But, it's Christmas eve ... I know ... all right ... I'll see you in a bit ... bye.

(GRACE hangs up phone and NICK enters from bedroom with gift. He sits on couch waiting and silent.)

GRACE: Ginny says that Malcolm is freaking out about the show tomorrow. He wants to run through the Mendelssohn piece one more time. I should be back by 10:00. It's still Christmas Eve till midnight ...

(NICK doesn't answer. GRACE puts gift in front of him and awkwardly takes her gift. NICK ignores the gifts and continues to drink directly from the bottle.)

GRACE: *(Opening gift.)* Oh look, a Christmas tree topper. Let's put it on the tree. *(GRACE places topper on tree.)*

NICK: You're fucking Malcolm, the conductor aren't you?

GRACE: Excuse me?

NICK: The man on the phone? That was Malcolm, wasn't it?

GRACE: Oh my God.

NICK: *(Mimicking man on phone.)* I have to see you ... I've been thinking about you all day ...

GRACE: Stop it!

NICK: You are so cliché. A soloist fucking the conductor!

GRACE: I refuse to try and reason with an intoxicated person. I'm going to stay at Ginny's house tonight. Maybe we can talk about this like grownups in the morning.

NICK: Hold on! You think your gonna just waltz on outta here and go meet your lover! On Christmas Eve? Oh no lady, you're not going anywhere!

(GRACE brushes past him and exits to bedroom, off-stage right. NICK paces in front of bedroom door, drinking and fuming. GRACE appears in doorway wearing a coat and carrying a small duffel bag. NICK jumps in front of her blocking her path.)

GRACE: C'mon Nick, don't be an asshole. Let me by.

NICK: Do you love him?

GRACE: I'm not going to do this now.

NICK: Do you love me?

GRACE: It's not that simple.

NICK: Explain it to me.

GRACE: I'm pregnant!

NICK: What?! Whoa! Let me get this straight. You begged me to get a vasectomy so you could stop taking the pill. And now you're knocked up with another man's baby? This is unbelievable! I thought you didn't even want kids!

GRACE: I didn't. I don't. I can't believe that I'm actually pregnant!

NICK: Well now-and-days, there are ways to become un-pregnant you know?

GRACE: See that's the thing. I've been thinking about it and …

NICK: And what?

GRACE: And I don't think I can go through with it. Did you know that the baby's heart starting beating at six weeks?

NICK: Wait just a minute! You're not actually considering having this baby? Another man's baby? There is no way in hell that I am going to let that happen!

GRACE: *(Slowly and deliberately.)* Well Nick, there are some things in life that you have absolutely no control over.

(NICK and GRACE stare at each, challenging the other to make a move. Finally NICK grudgingly lets her pass to the front door. NICK pulls his gun and points it at her back. As she passes the Christmas tree, the lights go down. Gunshot. GRACE crumples to floor, pulling the Christmas tree down with her. NICK uprights the tree and replaces the tree topper. Christmas tree lights off.)

SCENE VI

(Lights up. Back to the present. NICK is still standing in front of the Christmas tree. He takes the topper down and stares at it. There is a loud knock at the door.)

NICK: *(Opening door.)* What now?

(Lights down. The audience can not see who is at the door.)

(The End)

Denise Collins as MOTHER, Tim Eliot as SON
and Matt Hanley as DAD in THIS QUIET HOUSE in
The Riant Theatre's Strawberry One-Act Festival Winter 2008
at The American Theater of Actors in NYC

THIS QUIET HOUSE

By Toby Levin

Toby Levin is a graduate of Bennington College, where he studied playwriting with Catherine Filloux and Caridad Svich. His play *La Corraleja* was a 2006 finalist for the Heideman Award. He performed his Spanish-language solo piece *El acto final*, based on the life and works of Federico García Lorca, at Bennington in the spring of 2006.

This Quiet House debuted on February 16, 2008 as part of The Riant Theatre's Winter 2008 Strawberry One-Act Festival at the American Theatre of Actors, where it was a semi-finalist. It was performed with the following cast, in order of appearance:

MOTHER	Denise Collins
FATHER	Matt Hanley
SON	Tim Eliot

The play was directed by Lucy Skeen, with sound design by Ryan Biracree.

CAST OF CHARACTERS

MOTHER, 50's, gray hair, a woman of intense passions and a vivid imagination.
FATHER, 50's, muscular, gray hair, a man with a powerful presence and a body to match.
SON, early 20's, a young man with an attractive intensity and a strong memory.

(Note: "Wee, wee" is the sound of a pig's squeal. It is also the sound of a child's excited scream. These two uses should both be used to a lesser or greater extent. However, by the end of the play every "wee, wee" should sound like a pig.)

(A kitchen that is also a straw-covered pig sty, also the sunset. MOTHER is cleaning, washing dishes, cleaning counters, etc.)

MOTHER: Here. Here my husband will cook dinner. My big man, broad-shouldered, a farmer in the fields. A pitchfork, dusty jeans, the red, red sunset. He will cook for me. I'm the lucky lady, sitting on the lawn. Parasol and lacy sundress, ready for my picnic. Flush with the heat. But I want, I want. I am no mother. I am no mother, just a step-, a step-mother. A son of my own. I was a little girl in the garden: carrots, turnips, tomatoes, and I wanted a son. My husband's son, his mother left long ago, when all of us were young, before I even knew this man. His son is a man now: broad shoulders and a face. Hail on a forest. That man … No. He's a boy. Just a boy with a boy's face and his father's body. I want a son, my son. I want him in my arms, from my body. But this man, boy works a magic. He is an animal, a wild animal. The farmer raised him tame, but he is wild, wild. *(A change: she is on alert.)* He's here. I feel it under my skin like a bruise creeping into my breasts. I need it. I need him. I have always wanted a son. My husband the farmer tells me that sows will eat piglets that aren't their own. A piglet strays from its mother's teat in the pen. Wee, wee. Wee, wee. The only thing it's ever known is the pink warmth of its mother's stomach and the struggle for milk. A pink comes up out of the straw. It doesn't smell like mother, but the warmth is the same. The belly is the same. The pink is the same. Wee, wee. My husband grew up on a farm, saw it every day. Wee, wee. Where's Mama? Where's my mama? Wee, wee. Wee, wee.

(FATHER enters.)

FATHER: Talking to yourself again?

MOTHER: Why not?

FATHER: No reason. You sound like honey.

MOTHER: Quiet. I'll be quiet, too.

FATHER: I'd rather make you scream.

MOTHER: Stop it.

FATHER: I'd rather make you moan and claw. Make you kick your feet in the air. Make your eyes roll back until only the whites are showing.

MOTHER: I've been cleaning.

FATHER: Every husband wants the maid.

MOTHER: You are my husband.

FATHER: And you're the maid.

MOTHER: No, I've been cleaning.

FATHER: You've been cleaning my kitchen, my house. It's my house you're cleaning.

(They fuck passionately.)

MOTHER: Just one thing. I love you, I love you. But I'm old. I'm old. I'm a mother. A mother and no child. Oh, I love you. I love you.

FATHER: I love you.

MOTHER: I love you. You make an animal of me. You. You! You make an animal. You make me, make me. Oh, you animal. I am old. I ...

FATHER: You are an animal.

MOTHER: I am a mother now and no child. No child, but I love you. You. Animal. Ah, ah animal. Ah. Ah.

(She kicks the air. Her eyes roll. She screams. They finish. A pause.)

FATHER: I love you.

MOTHER: There is something. I can feel it under my skin, moving through my body.

FATHER: I love you.

MOTHER: No. Something else.

FATHER: I love you.

MOTHER: I love you. But there is something else.

FATHER: What is it?

MOTHER: It lives under my skin. It creeps in like a slow fog then explodes. I don't know. It is a need, an itch that burns cold and sharp. I don't know. I don't know.

FATHER: Have you chopped the onions for dinner yet?

MOTHER: It creeps down into my breasts and sets a fire, a cold fire, icicles in my chest. You can't melt them. Who can melt them? Do you know?

FATHER: I'm as warm as anyone else. Am I not enough?

MOTHER: I love you. But there is a need, a need.

FATHER: I'm not enough.

MOTHER: No. You are enough. I love you. But I want things, too. No, no. I love you. I love you. I'll chop the onions.

FATHER: Call for me when you're done.

(FATHER exits. MOTHER chops onions.)

MOTHER: The farmer-animal-lover in the hay. He always cries when there are onions. Like a baby. My baby. Even if he's cooking, I have to chop the onions. I have strong eyes, long lashes. The only woman in this house of men. Making bread as I sip my tea. All around me big strong trees that never notice the winds and storms. But my eyes are strong. *(On alert like before.)* I can feel him. He's here. I can feel him. Even through the haze of onions, getting ready for dinner. And I am the only woman this house will see. My mother told me a good wife gets dinner ready without letting the house go. I am a good wife, a good mother. The house is always put together and dinner always ready. But I want my own. My own. Where are my babies tugging on my apron? What have I done? I need him. Where are they, running a chaos around me while I cook? This is a quiet house! I need my son. I need him racing, screaming, crying out, strong eyes or no. I need him. I need him. No. No. My eyes are strong, long lashes. Just like my mother's. He should be crawling at my feet, distracting me, making me laugh. I should cry on his cheeks when he falls. I have been good with my life and now I live in this quiet house. What have I done? No, no. My eyes are strong. Strong eyes with my mother's long lashes. Long, long lashes.

(SON enters.)

SON: Wee, wee. Wee, wee. My mother left me for a far off land. Long black hair and thick eyebrows, all I can remember. The scent of apples and onions. My mother left me and my father for a far off land. He doesn't remember, tries not to remember. She was tall, big thighs, long black hair and thick eyebrows. We used to pull in our legs and say that we were snails, inching across the floor. We used to draw pictures of the sun setting in a cloudless sky. Then one day after dinner she was gone. An empty space at the table. The dishes still dirty in the sink and no one to tuck us into bed. Where are you, Mama? Where is your long black hair, your freckled arms? You left and died a cloud's disappearing death. Mama? Mama, when I ate your death, I licked my lips and got lost in it. It dribbled down my chin and perhaps left a stain on my shirt. I was how old? Only that old? You smelled like apples and onions, but that's not how you tasted. Meaty, juices dribbling down my chin and perhaps staining my shirt. Wild and gamey. When I ate your death, I was seated calmly with a red napkin. I licked my lips and got lost in it.

MOTHER: I already chopped the onions.

SON: What else could I do? Your death and I ate, got lost in it. Let it dribble down my chin, stain my shirt. I licked my lips. What else could I do?

MOTHER: But dinner won't be ready for a while. Your father is cooking.

SON: What's for dinner?

MOTHER: I need him to cook sometimes. You don't know how age will wear you out. Even standing is sometimes more than I can handle.

SON: You're not old yet. Old enough to be my mother, but not old yet.

MOTHER: *(As a child.)* When I am young, I draw pictures of cows and sheep in a field. I draw pictures of the ocean full of fish and whales. The daytime sky always has some clouds. In my imagination, it does. Two clouds here, one cloud there, but the sun is always shining. I have no babies. I draw pictures of the sunset. The pinks spill onto my dress and I am a princess. I have no babies.

SON: I am your son now.

MOTHER: *(Still a child.)* Where do we live? On the tops of snowy mountains. Where the sun never burns. It floats over green grass. We are always pink, pink, pink like pigs, pigs, pigs. My mama makes us strawberries with cream and powdered sugar. We wear high-heels with diamonds and lacy straps. My mama wears a sun dress every day because it's too hot to wear anything else. She smells like onions when she's sweaty.

SON: You are my mother now.

MOTHER: *(As a woman.)* I'm not you're mother. She left long ago.

SON: But now. I miss her apples and onions, the way she smelled. The soft skin on her inner arms. The two freckles on her jaw. Her big thighs, long black hair. But now. I'm hungry.

MOTHER: Where is your father? My old bones are getting hungry.

SON: It's getting late.

MOTHER: *(Calling to Father.)* I cut the onions.

(FATHER enters.)

FATHER: Safe?

MOTHER: It's safe.

FATHER: I watched the sunrise this morning. Your snoring welcomed in the day. Russet, red, scarlet, the pink and my breath became the same as yours, sawing into the walls on the inhale. Didn't you know you snore? Don't look at me that way.

SON: Father, I'm here.

FATHER: I watched the blue flood onto the sky as the pink disappeared. Your snores took off the walls until I could feel the chill of dawn. Don't look like that. You knew. I love you, that's all. You knew. We've talked about it before.

SON: Father, I'm here.

FATHER: *(Noticing his son for the first time.)* Are you getting hungry? It's getting so late.

SON: I can wait.

MOTHER: I can cook; I'm not so old.

FATHER: No, no. I'll cook. We'll have the pork chops we bought. I'll cook the onions, now that it's safe. Pork chops with sweet roasted onions.

MOTHER: *(As a child.)* I draw the sunset on a cloudless day and the pink spills on my mother's sun dress. Have you seen the summer breeze? It's turned green like a gopher, I mean frog. Green like a frog and my mother wears a pink sundress. I have no children, no babies at all.

FATHER: We have a son, my dear.

MOTHER: *(As a woman.)* I have no children.

FATHER: *(To Son.)* Put the pork chops in the oven for me.

SON: I hope they're not too gamey.

MOTHER: No. You'll like them. With the sweet onions dripping their juices.

FATHER: Running down your chin and dripping onto your shirt. Leaving a sweet onion stain across your breast pocket.

SON: No. Do I have some time?

FATHER: I'll do the cooking.

SON: I have a thing to do. My mother left me for a far off land.

(SON exits.)

MOTHER: Wait! He's not my child. I feel it like a bruise under my skin, creeping down into my breasts. I can feel it, milk it from my nipples like a juice. Wee, wee. My mother wore a sun dress and fed us strawberries.

FATHER: Your breathing was the sound of the earth moving, my love. Didn't you know?

MOTHER: I know.

FATHER: This morning when the sun came up.

MOTHER: I know. He's still here.

FATHER: I watched the sun come up and listened to you snore. It could only have been you.

MOTHER: The pork chops. My bones are tired.

FATHER: I know. I'm cooking.

(The movements of cooking: vegetables, potatoes, the oven. MOTHER sits, feeling her age.)

MOTHER: I was a girl with a garden and long, long hair. Now I've grown and where is the sunset? Is there really no sunset? I loved a young man with a head of red curls. I grew vegetables in my garden and we ate them, the young man with red curls and I. I grew radishes and beets, peppers and tomatoes. I grew onions, sharp and sweet and the boy with red curls. I loved him. Now, I have grown. What if there is no sunset, really? What if there is never a sunset? I grew onions. I had long, long hair and I believed in the sunset. I thought it would fade, and fade brightly. But it never flared up. It was reaching white and then suddenly black, never bright in the sky, never a glorious display so you could forget the fading. It was slow and then quickly it was over. I thought I was watching the sunset sometimes. I thought I could see the brilliant reds and oranges, but now where is the sunset? It was beautiful, spectacular even. But was it ever the sunset? Was it never the sunset? My hair is growing white and I am old.

FATHER: No, you're beautiful.

MOTHER: We're getting old.

FATHER: Together. *(Beat.)* The food is ready.

MOTHER: Where is your son?

FATHER: You are his mother.

MOTHER: No. His mother left for a far off land. We haven't heard from her in years. I sometimes want a son.

FATHER: We're getting old together. Let's eat.

MOTHER: I always want a son. I am too old to have a child, but I want to have one. A son to hold and press to my flesh. A son to brush and to love and to sing to. You have a son of your own. Your flesh. Your blood. But he's not mine. Do you know? I want to know what it feels like to start a life. I want to know what it means to grow a seed inside me. I want to watch my belly grow and not care about fat. Do you know? You can't hear me. I am old. I am too old, but I need a son of my own. I need him, mine. I am hungry. Do you know? Don't you know? No. You can't hear me. We are happy. You have a son of your own. We are happy in our quiet house. Only a woman … No, no. It's okay. No. You can't hear me. Where is your son?

FATHER: Mother?

MOTHER: Where is your son?

FATHER: I'll call for him.

MOTHER: No. We'll wait. Sit. The food is ready.

(They sit. A silence.)

FATHER: Mother?

MOTHER: No.

FATHER: I'll give you a son.

MOTHER: No. I am an old woman. Too old for children of my own.

FATHER: But your body is …

MOTHER: I am old. Where is your son?

FATHER: He'll come back. Let's eat.

MOTHER: We'll wait.

FATHER: We're getting old. Together.

MOTHER: We'll wait.

FATHER: I grew up with pigs. You hear "pigs," think piglets, pink and clean. Happy faces, big snouts, pointed ears. I think sharp teeth, cloven hooves, pork chops. And the smell. Pigs smell. It's really not the pigs themselves, they're clean. It's their shit. Did you know that the intestines of a pig are the same as the intestines of a man? Their shit smells like man shit. Everywhere. My childhood was the smell of pig shit on the wind. Every day it was in my room when I woke up and in my room when I went to sleep. Unless there was a west wind. My house was on the west side of the pig barns. The west wind was my savior. I think that was why I loved his mother. The west wind was her savior, too. She couldn't resist it.

MOTHER: That's why she left?

FATHER: The west wind. I try not to remember. Now when I see pork chops, I thank the west wind and go crazy. It's a victory. Their shit lost to my hunger. When I eat their death, I lick my lips and get lost in it.

MOTHER: You are an animal.

FATHER: We both are.

MOTHER: You are a crazed animal. Mad with blood lust. Where is your son?

FATHER: He'll be here.

MOTHER: He needed time. Do we have time?

FATHER: The food is ready.

MOTHER: We're waiting. I'm not a mother.

FATHER: You're the maid.

MOTHER: Yes. You are an animal.

FATHER: Yes. I am a crazed animal. Come.

MOTHER: No. Stay away. You're crazy.

FATHER: Come to me.

MOTHER: I need …

FATHER: Hush. I need to taste your flesh, your meat.

MOTHER: You animal.

(They fuck passionately again.)

MOTHER: Maybe. Maybe I am not too old.

FATHER: You are beautiful. You make me an animal.

MOTHER: I am no mother. I am an animal. An animal, crazed. I have no child. My body needs it. I need it. Give it to me. Give it to me.

FATHER: You are an animal. A wild, wild animal.

MOTHER: I need it. I need it. A mother. Give it to me. A mother. Give. Give. Give. A mother. A mother. I love you.

(They finish.)

FATHER: Now I'm hungry.

MOTHER: You are an animal, but you are still a man. Where is your son?

FATHER: He is our son. He'll come.

MOTHER: We'll wait. You are hungry.

FATHER: You are beautiful.

MOTHER: Where is he?

FATHER: We'll wait.

(SON enters.)

SON: There is a fire. I dropped a candle on the bed and it's on fire.

FATHER: Where were you?

SON: I dropped a fire on the candle and it's on the bed.

MOTHER: There is a fire? There is a fire now?

SON: I dropped the bed on fire and there is a candle.

MOTHER: Get water. Get some water!

(MOTHER runs out.)

FATHER: Where were you?

SON: On the bed. I don't know what it was. There is a fire now and I can't put it out.

FATHER: I was hungry. The food is ready and we were waiting.

SON: My mother left for a far off land and I was thinking as the candle dropped how she always spoke of the west wind. I opened up the window as the candle dropped onto the bed. It was on fire and there was a west wind coming through the curtains. It was her savior. Do you know? You forget. And now the candle is on fire in the bed.

FATHER: The west wind was my savior. We fell in love. I try to forget now that she's gone. We were waiting.

SON: The west wind came in the window and then the candle down, down, down. Boom.

(FATHER runs out.)

SON: There is a fire. You are the man, Father. I never forget my mother. I never forget to light a candle and send it to her on the west wind. The west wind was her savior. It is still her savior. She couldn't resist, I know. And now there is a fire. For you, Father. Now it's for you. *(He sits and eats.)* My father is a forgetful man. Forgetting all the time. I remember my mother: tall, a strong laugh, two small freckles on her jaw. She smelled like onions. Like a pork chop baked with sweet onions in a hot oven. There is a fire, that I will always remember. She was a strong woman, I know, and I was a young boy. My father can't remember, won't remember. This is a delicious pork chop. Tonight, I will be a man, but I am still a boy. Wee, wee. A little boy, too young to know a thing. Wee, wee. Wee, wee. *(As a child.)* Father and Mother don't know what I'm doing. They eat chocolate and lock their door. Wee, wee. I can't hear you. I can't hear you. Father and Mother are taking a nap. I'm taking a nap, too. They think so. But I'm hungry. There is a ham sandwich with my name on it. Yum. In the refrigerator, it's cold, but I don't mind. I like it with mayonnaise and mustard. Wee, wee. They think I'm asleep, but I am eating my ham sandwich. I can't hear you. I can't hear you.

(The fire is beginning to become apparent: a red glow from one side of the stage.)

SON: *(Still a child.)* My sandwich tastes so good. It gives me an itch in my belly and it moves. The itch moves and it wants me to touch it, to scratch it. It moves down, down, down and I need to touch it. The sandwich is gone and the itch is everything. I need to touch it. I can't hear you. I can't hear you. I need to touch it. So I do. It feels like butter melting on toast. I can taste it in my mouth and my pants are on fire, warm and glowing. It feels good. Wee, wee. Wee, wee. I feel like butter melting on toast. Mother and Father have the door locked and are taking a nap. I am, too. I am, too. The itch is gone, it's a fire. It's a fire and I'm warm and glowing like butter and butter and my ham sandwich. The mustard is burning and I love it. I can't hear you. Wee, wee. I can't hear you.

(He has fallen onto the floor, overwhelmed. The fire has clearly grown. MOTHER runs in, sweaty.)

MOTHER: The fire. Your father. We need help with the fire.

SON: *(As himself.)* What?

MOTHER: Your father is at the fire. Wee, wee need help.

SON: My father.

MOTHER: Needs help. We need to get help.

SON: Will stop the fire. Father. He is a man.

MOTHER: Get help!

SON: We are safe. Father will stop the fire. He is a man, broad-shouldered and strong. We are safe.

MOTHER: There is a fire.

SON: I can't hear you. Wee, wee.

MOTHER: You stay here. I am your mother now. You stay here and I will help him. My son, my son.

SON: No, no. I started the fire but you need to eat.

MOTHER: Hush. Wee, wee.

SON: We are okay. Father is fighting the fire. He is a big, big man. I have a fire, warm and glowing like butter melting on toast. I have an itch, moves down, down, down.

MOTHER: Your fire? Wee, wee need help.

SON: Wee, wee need help with my fire.

MOTHER: Like butter melting on toast. Down, down, down.

SON: Down, down, down.

MOTHER: Hush. The big, big man is fighting the fire. The big, big man, we are safe. I am hungry, your mother.

SON: Dinner is on the table.

MOTHER: No. Did you eat?

SON: Are you hungry?

MOTHER: Did you eat?

SON: Are you hungry?

(They fall into each other on the floor. Rabid, animalistic sex that is also like a mother caring for her son. She suckles him, pig-like. The entire room is glowing from the fire.)

MOTHER: My son. My son is here. I am a mother. Yes, with a child. I love you. A child and a mother and I love you. Wee, wee. Wee, wee. I am an animal in the hay. An animal I love you.

SON: Wee, wee. Wee, wee.

MOTHER: I am a mother with a son. My own son, I love you. You. You.

SON: Wee, wee.

MOTHER: An animal, a mother with a child. My own son, I love you.

(FATHER enters, sweaty, sooty, with a pitchfork. MOTHER and SON don't notice.)

FATHER: The fire. I can't. The fire.

MOTHER: Wee, wee.

FATHER: Mother. My son.

MOTHER: Wee, wee. I love you.

FATHER: I grew up on a farm, saw it every day. Sows will eat piglets that aren't their own. A piglet strays from it's mother's teat in the pen. The only thing it's ever known is the pink warmth of its mother's stomach.

SON: Wee, wee.

FATHER: You think piglets, pink and clean. I think sharp teeth, cloven hooves. Pork chops and the smell. Pigs smell. It's their shit.

SON: Wee, wee.

FATHER: And the struggle for milk. A new pink comes up in the straw. It doesn't smell like mother, but the warmth is the same.

MOTHER: Wee, wee.

FATHER: My childhood was the smell of pig shit on the wind. Every day it was in my room when I woke up and in my room when I went to sleep. Unless there was a west wind.

SON: Wee, wee.

MOTHER: Wee, wee. I love you.

FATHER: I grew up on a farm, saw it every day.

(FATHER skewers MOTHER and SON with his pitchfork. A brief, squirming death. FATHER sits at the table, eats.)

FATHER: When I ate your death, I licked my lips and got lost in it. It dribbled down my chin and perhaps left a stain on my shirt. I was how old? I was that old? You smelled like apples and onions, but that's not how you tasted. Meaty, juices dribbling down my chin and perhaps staining my shirt. Wild and gamey. When I ate your death, I was seated calmly with a red napkin. I licked my lips and got lost in it. And the west wind. The west wind, my savior since my childhood in my room that smelled like pig shit on the farm where I grew up. I saw it every day. I saw it every day. I got lost in it. I was a farmer-animal-lover in the hay. And now

I'm what? Now what am I? There is no sunset really. It fades, but not brightly. It never flares up. It's reaching white and then it is suddenly black, never bright like the sunset, never a glorious display so you forget the fading and the loss. It is slow and then quickly it is over. My hair is going gray. I am barely a man these days. But the west wind is still my savior. I cannot resist and I cannot forget. I try to forget, am forgetful, but I cannot forget. The smell. I smelled it every day. When I ate your death, I licked my lips and got lost in it. It dribbled down my chin and left a bright red stain on my shirt. I was seated calmly with a red napkin. I licked my lips and got lost in it.

(The fire consumes the room as FATHER finishes his pork chop.)

(The End)

Matt Dunnam as MADISON, Alison Rabiej as HANNAH, Zach Harvey as JAMES,
David J. Hommel as ADDISON, Laura Harrison as EVA
and Tim Torres (Kneeling) as MAN WITH THE NICE COLLARD SHIRT
in WHAT CHEER, IOWA in
The Riant Theatre's Strawberry One-Act Festival Winter 2008
at The American Theater of Actors in NYC

WHAT CHEER, IOWA
By Jeff Belanger

Jeff Belanger graduated with a BFA in Dramatic Writing from SUNY Purchase's Theater Arts & Film Conservatory. He is one of the three founding members of the International Brain Transplant Committee. Jeff usually tries his best to do a lot of different things in a lot of different places.

What Cheer, Iowa made its New York City debut on February 16th, 2008 at The American Theatre of Actors. It was a finalist in The Riant Theatre's Winter 2008 Strawberry One-Act Festival winning "Best Actor" (Zach Harvey) and "Best Director" (Sean Kenealy). It was performed with the following cast, in order of appearance:

JAMES	Zach Harvey
EVA	Laura Harrison
ADDISON	David J. Hommel
HANNAH	Alison Rabiej
MAN WITH THE NICE COLLARED SHIRT	Tim Torres
MADISON	Matt Dunnam

The play was directed by Sean Kenealy.

CAST OF CHARACTERS:

JAMES, male, forty.
EVA, female, forty.
ADDISON, male, mid-twenties.
HANNAH, female, early twenties.
MAN WITH THE NICE COLLARED SHIRT, male, any age.
MADISON, male, mid-twenties.

(A tacky picture of a car hangs on the bland, bland, bland gray wall. Signs with bold lettering are posted around the picture, one of which reads "PLEASE TAKE ALL VALUABLES WHEN EXITING YOUR VEHICLE." Four people stand behind a bright orange plastic construction fence. They all look extremely nervous and restless. JAMES, forty and moustached, is biting the nails on one hand and the other is attached to an old floor lamp. EVA, thirty, holds her hands on her hips and is staring off, gape mouthed, thinking deeply about something. ADDISON, mid twenties, wearing a nice suit, is clutching a safety deposit box and reading a Men's magazine. HANNAH, twenty, is juggling an iPod, a cell phone, a small television, and a laptop. She is listening to music too loudly to hear most of the conversation. James, perhaps in an attempt to stave off his restlessness, meanders over to Addison.)

JAMES: Hi, my name's James.

ADDISON: Addison.

JAMES: Nice to meetcha.

(James and Addison shake hands.)

JAMES: Which one is yours?

ADDISON: Hmm?

JAMES: Which one is yours?

ADDISON: Oh, the silver one.

(Addison points offstage. James whistles.)

JAMES: Nice car.

ADDISON: Yeah.

JAMES: That's a fine car.

ADDISON: That's why I bought it.

JAMES: What year is it?

ADDISON: 2006.

JAMES: How many miles?

ADDISON: 5,308.4.

(James nods approvingly. Addison points offstage.)

ADDISON: That's your truck?

JAMES: That's ma baby.

ADDISON: Holds up all right?

JAMES: It's holds up all right, all right.

(James laughs and claps his hands. Addison smiles.)

ADDISON: I bet you're a man that takes care of his vehicle.

JAMES: You bet right. I tell ya, I had gotten divorced just a month after I bought this car. Hannah wanted—Her name's Hannah—she wanted the car as a part of the settlement and I knew she couldn't take care of a nice car like that although it was a lot nicer when I first bought it.

ADDISON: Most things are.

JAMES: Sure are. And well, I'd be damned if that woman got her mitts on the car, letting it fall apart. Not getting the proper tune ups and what have you. Sure was a messy divorce though. A lot of screaming and crying.

(Addison nods.)

JAMES: I cried. I'm not past admitting that. I cried a lot during the whole ... thing.

ADDISON: Well, at least you can admit it.

JAMES: Hard divorce. It was really hard on me.

ADDISON: Yeah, they sure look hard. Divorce Court and all ...

JAMES: Yeah, Divorce sure is big now. Everyone I know is getting one. It's selling like hot cakes ...

(James chuckles.)

ADDISON: Divorce really isn't sold, though.

JAMES: Yeah, it sells itself.

ADDISON: Ha ... well ...

JAMES: I just didn't want her ruining my nice car.

ADDISON: Yeah, you look like a man who takes care of his car.

JAMES: Looks don't deceive.

(Addison eyes James.)

ADDISON: You mind if I ask a personal question?

JAMES: About my divorce?

ADDISON: About your car.

(James narrows his eyes.)

JAMES: Go ahead.

ADDISON: You think it'll pass?

JAMES: What?

ADDISON: You think your car will pass?

JAMES: What? You don't think it'll pass?

ADDISON: No, I'm—

JAMES: You don't think it'll pass!!!

ADDISON: NO! I mean, yeah! I meant "No, I'm not implying that it won't pass."

JAMES: Then why're you asking?

ADDISON: I ... I—I ...

JAMES: What kind of man goes around asking people if they think their cars are going to pass inspection?

ADDISON: I DIDN—

JAMES: WHY I OUGHTA—

(Eva intervenes.)

EVA: Hey now! What's all this ruckus?

JAMES: This man's a sonuvabitch!

ADDISON: I didn't mean anything!

EVA: What'd you do?

JAMES: He asked me if I thought my car would pass inspection!

EVA: Oh.

ADDISON: I wasn't implying anything.

EVA: Why would you ask him that?

ADDISON: I asked if it was okay!

JAMES: That don't make it right. That don't make it right …

ADDISON: I'm sorry! He was talking about how much he cried and I thought maybe it'd be all right.

JAMES: I don't know what kind of person you are, but I don't go around talking like that. That's just …

EVA: Sick.

JAMES: That's not how people should behave in public.

EVA: It's sick.

JAMES: That's not what decent folk talk about.

ADDISON: I don't know what I was thinking! I'm sorry.

JAMES: Well, "Sorry" don't make it better.

ADDISON: Listen …

(Addison opens his box and takes out a handful of money.)

ADDISON: Lemme give you some money.

(James grabs the money and puts it in his pocket.)

JAMES: All right. But only because I'm so steamed.

ADDISON: I'm sorry.

JAMES: Just so goddamned steamed. You got more money in that box?

ADDISON: … What?

JAMES: You heard me. I ain't interested in your money. I just wanna know why you're carrying it around.

ADDISON: They said to take all the valuables out of the car.

JAMES: And that's what you took?

ADDISON: It's awfully valuable to me.

JAMES: Yeah, if I had a box I really liked, I'd probably wanna put money in it too.

(Addison regards James strangely.)

JAMES: I took my lamp.

(James demonstrates his lamp. Addison and Eva regard his lamp.)

EVA: Hey, that's a really great lamp.

JAMES: My name's James.

EVA: I'm Eva.

(James and Eva shake hands.)

ADDISON: Addison.

EVA: Eva.

(Addison and Eva shake hands.)

JAMES: I'm divorced.

EVA: I'm very sorry.

JAMES: That's how I got this lamp here.

EVA: Someone gave it to you cause they felt bad?

JAMES: Nah, I got in the settlement. My Divorce settlement. I also got that truck. And some sheets and a bag of plastic bags and a small television and a spider plant and a smaller spider plant and a cutting board and a pet mouse but he died.

EVA: That's quite a haul.

JAMES: Yeah, it made the whole thing worth it. Didn't you have any valuables in your car?

EVA: Lunch.

JAMES: What?

EVA: My sandwich. It's in the car.

ADDISON: You left it in the car?!

EVA: I thought … maybe … it'd be all right. It's in the glove compartment.

ADDISON: Brave.

EVA: Brave? Why's that brave? They're not gonna—

ADDISON: No, no. I'm sorry to worry you. It'll probably be fine.

EVA: You think?

(Addison nods half-heartedly.)

EVA: They're gonna touch my sandwich, aren't they?

EVA: Ham. Ham Sandwich. I can't imagine that guy with the nice red collared shirt is gonna want anything to do with a ham sandwich … He better not at least.

JAMES: Ham Sandwich, that's a good truck drivin' sandwich. I should know.

EVA: You're truck driver?

JAMES: Certainly am. I've carried lumber around in my truck to all fifty states of this great nation—

ADDISON: Forty-nine.

JAMES: FIFTY! There's fifty states of this great nation!

ADDISON: But you can't drive to all of 'em in your truck.

JAMES: GOD DAMN IT! You say one more thing about my truck and I'll punch you in the throat! I can do anything in my truck!

ADDISON: Listen, I'm not trying to insult your truck or anything, I'm just saying you can't DRIVE to Hawaii!

JAMES: I can and I will and I'll do it again!

EVA: All right now, calm down! CALM DOWN! Jeez, you guys. This is a stressful enough situation as is. Can't you just agree to disagree?

ADDISON: How!?

JAMES: What does that even mean?

EVA: It means, James, you admit that its impossible to drive to all fifty states but, Addison, you have to agree that James has done it and will probably do it again.

(Silence.)

ADDISON: Yeah, all right.

JAMES: I'm fine with that.

(Hannah scoffs. James looks in her direction.)

JAMES: And you are?

HANNAH: Yes?

(Hannah takes her headphones off.)

JAMES: What's yer name?

HANNAH: Why?

JAMES: Well, we've all gotten to know each other 'cept …

HANNAH: Sorry, I already know a lot of people. I'm good.

EVA: Then why were you listening to our conversation?

HANNAH: Oh, my 30GB Apple iPod classic AAC/MP3 Video Player was between tracks so I caught that last bit.

(Addison stares at Hannah.)

ADDISON: You look awfully familiar. What's your name?

HANNAH: Hannah.

JAMES: You have the same name as my ex-wife.

ADDISON: Do you work around here?

HANNAH: Nope.

JAMES: Lemme tell you a story about my ex-wif—

ADDISON: What bank do you belong to?

HANNAH: Crest National.

EVA: Like the toothpaste?

HANNAH: Like the bank.

EVA: It's a toothpaste too.

HANNAH: I know.

ADDISON: It's also an accounting firm in—HEY! I know where I know you from!

HANNAH: Oh?

ADDISON: Kelly Harrison's party!

HANNAH: Uhhh …

ADDISON: You don't remember me?

HANNAH: Are you one of my Myspace friends?

ADDISON: I barely recognize you. I beat the shit out of you once!

(Hannah puts her hands on her hips.)

HANNAH: Did you?

ADDISON: Yeah! How could I forget you? You tore my nipple off!

HANNAH: I remember you now!

ADDISON: This is so funny!

(Addison and Hannah share a laugh.)

ADDISON: Man, that night, I got some bum Ruffies. Never got anything from that guy again. You were supposed to be sedated, you can imagine my surprise when you ripped my nipple off.

HANNAH: Yeah, I'm sorry about that whole nipple thing … but you know how it is.

ADDISON: Oh, its no big deal. Just a worthless old nipple. I shoulda ripped it off years ago. Wasn't getting me anywhere.

HANNAH: I'll bet! So what have you been up to? I haven't seen you at any of the hip parties I go to.

ADDISON: Oh, I don't really run that circuit anymore.

HANNAH: That's a shame. Why not?

ADDISON: Well, you know, got a little older, lose interest.

HANNAH: You quit beating up women?

ADDISON: No, I don't try to like people anymore.

HANNAH: I'm sorry.

ADDISON: No, it's fine. I've made some great headway since.

(Addison gestures to his safety deposit box. A huge spotlight shines down onto Addison. Addison ducks down and covers his ears. A voice booms.)

VOICE: ADDISON HOLMES!

ADDISON: NO! I don't want to hear it!

VOICE: ADDISON HOLMES!

ADDISON: NO! NONONONONONONONONONONONONONON O! NO!

(Addison sobs a little. Then he screams.)

ADDISON: ALL RIGHT! TELL ME! TELL ME!

VOICE: Your car has finished inspection.

ADDISON: Please, God, no … God no …

VOICE: Your car has … passed.

(Addison looks up at the spotlight with tears streaming down his face. He's puffy and red and filled with emotion.)

ADDISON: Thank you. Thank you.

(James slowly claps soon followed by Eva. The clapping builds as Addison laughs joyously. Eva and James lift Addison to his feet.)

ADDISON: Oh thank god.

(A Man in a Nice Red Collared Shirt enters with a clipboard.)

MAN IN A NICE COLLARED SHIRT: Mr. Holmes?

(Addison weakly raises his hand and smiles.)

MAN IN A NICE COLLARED SHIRT: Congratulations, Mr. Holmes. If you could sign here and your sticker is already on your car.

ADDISON: This is a great day.

MAN IN A NICE COLLARED SHIRT: Yeah, it sure is.

(Addison gives the man a hug.)

MAN IN A NICE COLLARED SHIRT: Thank you.

ADDISON: No … thank you.

(Addison begins to exit.)

ADDISON: THANK YOU EVERYBODY!!!

(Addison runs off laughing. The Man looks off. James and Eva regard the man.)

JAMES: You just stand around and make people happy all day, don't you?

MAN IN A NICE COLLARED SHIRT: Sometimes … sometimes they don't pass though. And sometimes … I have to tazer people.

(The Man takes out a tazer. He looks real tough. Eva scoffs.)

JAMES: You have the best job in the world.

MAN IN A NICE COLLARED SHIRT: Thanks.

(The Man scribbles on the clipboard for a few more moments. James looks at Eva who has begun to stare off. The Man exits.)

EVA: What he said …

JAMES: Addison?

EVA: No, that man with the nice red collared shirt. The one who works here.

JAMES: What?

EVA: I keep thinking … what happens to the people who don't pass.

(James, wide eyed.)

HANNAH: They have to come back.

JAMES: WHAT?!

HANNAH: They have to get it fixed and come back to get it re-inspected.

(James smiles at Eva, he shakes his head.)
JAMES: Kids …
EVA: I keep thinking … what if I don't pass?
JAMES: Oh, don't—
EVA: No! I mean, everyone has to consider it. At least sometimes. What if my car isn't good enough? What if it's not the standard for which the rest of the cars are?
JAMES: I'm sure it's going to pass.
EVA: DON'T PATRONIZE ME, JAMES.
JAMES: I'm sorry. But I think—
EVA: No! Don't act like we can deny it. Someday … I may not pass inspection.
JAMES: So … like you said, everyone does.
EVA: But I'm not made of the same stuff as you and Hannah. I just can't come back. I can't drive around knowing that my car isn't good enough. I can feel it. It doesn't fit in. It's not good enough.
JAMES: I think you're thinking too much. Just distract yourself with—
(MADISON, male in his mid twenties, enters. He's carrying a bag of money with a dollar sign on it and wearing a suit almost identical to Addison's. James and Eva flip.)
JAMES: A NEW FRIEND!
EVA: What's your name?
MADISON: Uh … Madison.
(Everyone falls silent.)
JAMES: Huh.
MADISON: What?
EVA: It's strange.
MADISON: It's not that uncommon.
JAMES: The name? No.
MADISON: What is it?
JAMES: A man just left.
EVA: A friend.
JAMES: A man.
EVA: His name was Addison.
JAMES: And your name is Madison.
MADISON: Addison.
HANNAH: *(Jumping on his line.)* Madison.
MADISON: Yes?
(Hannah scoffs.)

EVA: Oh, she won't talk to you. She doesn't try. Not like us. What do you do?
MADISON: I'm a banker. I work at a bank.
EVA: That sounds so interesting.
MADISON: What do you do?
EVA: I'm a police negotiator.
JAMES: What?
MADISON: Oh.
(Eva explodes with laughter for two seconds then smiles.)
JAMES: Serious?
EVA: Yeah.
JAMES: Well, hot damn.
MADISON: Do you have a gun?
EVA: What kind of question is that? Of course I have a gun.
JAMES: Wouldn't be much of a cop without a gun.
MADISON: I thought maybe because you were a negotiator.
EVA: You know, sometimes, the gun does the negotiating for me.
(Eva takes out the gun. Everyone is impressed.)
EVA: Yeah, I know.
JAMES: So … show us something …
EVA: What?
JAMES: Negotiate something …
(Madison laughs.)
EVA: What? You think I can't do it?
MADISON: What? No, it's just … Nevermind.
EVA: What should I negotiate?
JAMES: I dunno. Anything.
(Eva points the gun at James. Madison immediately tenses up.)
MADISON: Uhh …
EVA: Come here.
(James smiles.)
JAMES: No.
(Eva smiles.)
EVA: Come here.
(A pause.)
JAMES: No.
(Madison laughs nervously. Eva cocks the gun.)
EVA: COME HERE, FUCKER!
(James automatically moves over to her. They stand within inches of each other. They stare at each other.)

HANNAH: Bang.

JAMES: God damn!

(James laughs uproariously. Eva smiles with satisfaction.)

JAMES: Well, god damn, woman! How'd you do that?

EVA: That's my job.

JAMES: That was great!

EVA: Did you see how I cocked the gun before I yelled real loud!?

JAMES: Yeah! I couldn't believe it! Negotiate Madison!

MADISON: NO!

EVA: Huh?

JAMES: Just let her do it, it's fun.

MADISON: It's insane!

JAMES: Why?

MADISON: I don't want her to point that thing at me!

EVA: Why not?

MADISON: It's a gun!

EVA: It's a tool of the trade.

MADISON: It's a deadly weapon!

JAMES: It's just a good time! Don't get like that, Madison. I thought we were friends.

MADISON: What? Why?

EVA: Because we're all under duress.

MADISON: So that means I should let you point a gun at me?

EVA: Yes!

JAMES: It encourages and strengthens bonds between us.

MADISON: How?

EVA: You're being very disruptive, Madison.

MADISON: Don't talk to me like that!!!

JAMES: You won't let us negotiate you.

MADISON: *(Pointing at Hannah.)* What about her?

JAMES: What about her?

MADISON: Why don't you negotiate her?

EVA: She doesn't want to.

MADISON: I don't want to either!

JAMES: She's not one of the team!

(Madison pauses.)

EVA: Is that what you're saying, Madison?

JAMES: You don't want to be with us?

MADISON: I just don't want to be threatened with a gun!

(Eva sighs and sits down onto the ground.)

EVA: I don't understand some people.

JAMES: Git out of here, Madison.

MADISON: What?

JAMES: I said "GIT!"

MADISON: I have to get my car inspected!

JAMES: Off our side!!

MADISON: What side?

(James points towards Hannah with a real serious face. Madison rolls his eyes and takes a few steps closer to Hannah.)

JAMES: Now you stay over there.

MADISON: Okay. *(To Hannah.)* What's their deal?

(Hannah just looks at him. Madison looks back. Hannah turns away. Madison makes a face. James walks over to Eva and soothes her.)

EVA: I don't understand it. Why does ... life ... have to be so hard?

JAMES: I don't know, Eva. Sometimes ... I don't know what the big guy up there has planned for us.

EVA: The guy that operates that spotlight?

JAMES: No, past him ...

(Eva looks confused.)

JAMES: God.

EVA: Ohhh ... yeah ... do you think maybe ... we should have embraced Madison with a loving ... embrace? Instead of pointing the gun at him.

JAMES: I dunno.

EVA: Like God is all about that kind of stuff, right?

JAMES: I'm not one of those God experts or anything. I just know ... I dunno ...

EVA: You can talk to me.

JAMES: I don't know nothing about loving embraces and whatnot. The only thing I know for sure ... I just know God gave me life and ... all this stuff. So he must want me to have all this stuff.

(James turns his lamp on and off.)

EVA: You think God is all right with us having guns?

JAMES: I think God wants us to have guns. Otherwise, why would they be here? I think he wants us to have guns and TVs and sandwiches and jeans and those little plush monkeys at drug stores, the ones with the Velcro arms so they can hug you.

EVA: And he must want us to have money too.

JAMES: Of course! Otherwise, how would we buy all the stuff he wants us to have!

EVA: What kind of God would he be if he didn't want us to be happy!?

JAMES: No God of mine, that's fer sure!

EVA: I think sometimes God just wants me to eat lots of bad food and spend money on cars have lots of sex and—and fire my gun up into the air and scream at children and old people who piss me off and sit around all day and watch movies and read magazines and have lots of sex … and …

(Eva looks into James' eyes.)

EVA: And have lots of sex …

(James looks deep.)

JAMES: Sometimes, I think God wants me to have lots of sex, too.

EVA: Do you really?

(James nods.)

JAMES: Sometimes … even … I think God wants … me to have lots of sex … uh … in the … the butt.

EVA: What?

JAMES: Like … to give … sex … sex in the butt …

EVA: Really?

JAMES: Sometimes.

EVA: I never think God wants me to get sex in the butt.

JAMES: Oh. I … I don't think he wants to me give it now, anyway. That's not what I think God wants now.

EVA: What does God want now?

(James gets very close. He whispers into Eva's ear. He looks at her. She nods. They both walk off stage. Madison stares off in horror.)

MADISON: That … that …

(Hannah turns to Madison.)

HANNAH: Listen, I'm not trying to have a conversation or …

MADISON: What?

HANNAH: Do I know you?

MADISON: I … I dunno …

HANNAH: Are you on Facebook?

MADISON: What's a Facebook?

HANNAH: Harrison Kelly's party!!

MADISON: Uhhh …

HANNAH: You probably don't remember me.

(Madison shakes his head.)

HANNAH: I beat the shit out of you once. I barely recognize you.

(Madison tilts his head.)
MADISON: Did you have a metal pipe?
HANNAH: Yeah, I tore it from underneath the sink!
MADISON: Oh my god! I can't believe this!
HANNAH: This is so funny!
(Madison and Hannah share a laugh.)
HANNAH: You know, I just ran into a guy that had beaten the shit out of me.
MADISON: Really?
HANNAH: Yeah, isn't that weird?
MADISON: Sure is. So what're you up to?
(The Man with the Nice Collared Shirt screams. James and Eva run onstage, pulling their clothes on with the Man following behind them.)
MAN IN A NICE COLLARED SHIRT: Every god damn day …
JAMES: We're sorry.
EVA: We won't do it again.
MAN IN A NICE COLLARED SHIRT: The disrespect is astounding. Don't you people have ANY shame?
JAMES: We didn't think you'd mind.
MAN IN A NICE COLLARED SHIRT: Listen, I work here. This is a place of business. Don't you understand that? This isn't a love shack. This isn't a little 'ole place where people can get together.
HANNAH: Love shack, baby.
MAN IN A NICE COLLARED SHIRT: SHUT UP. This isn't an easy job, you know! This isn't something I like doing everyday. I take this job VERY seriously. Everyday people come in here and I have to be the one to tell them whether or not their cars have passed inspection. Sure, people pass inspection more often than not, but do you know what its like to look someone in the eyes and tell that their car didn't pass inspection? Well? Do ya? Their eyes lose the little spark that lets you think that they're alive. Their skin turns translucent and wet. Their teeth fall out into little symmetric shapes on the ground! Their souls are sealed up, mailed away like so many Styrofoam peanuts of the heart! And their ears … oh, their ears … they dry … and wither … and fall to the ground … like leaves falling from a tree for the oncoming autumn. Little, gray ear-shaped leaves covering the ground of the garage. And outside … nothing. There's nothing outside.
EVA: Oh god.
JAMES: That clipboard. He carries around a million broken dreams with that clipboard.
EVA: It must be like a billion pounds or something.
JAMES: No one should have to carry that.

EVA: That's too heavy.

(There's a whole lot of silence. Madison stands uncomfortably.)

JAMES: Well, I'm bored.

EVA: I wonder why my car is taking so long to get inspected.

JAMES: Yeah ...

(Everyone looks at The Man. He looks up, tilts his head, and slowly angles it downward. Then he bends down and picks up his clipboard. The Man sighs and exits.)

EVA: Maybe we should've been nicer to him ...

JAMES: Well, we listened to his monologue.

EVA: That was pretty crazy.

JAMES: I didn't really pay attention.

EVA: I didn't get it. I feel bad ... maybe we should DO something?

JAMES: Like buy him a gift?

EVA: He's so ...

JAMES: Unfortunate.

EVA: I feel lucky, but that makes me feel so guilty.

JAMES: I feel so guilty.

EVA: I wish he'd never brought up that whole thing.

JAMES: Yeah, why couldn't he have just kept it to himself.

EVA: And not bothered us with it.

JAMES: He put that on us.

EVA: He's trying to make us feel bad!

JAMES: He's a sonuvabitch!

EVA: Especially since we're in this type of situation!

JAMES: We're under enough stress as is!

EVA: So much stress!

JAMES: I ... I can't believe he'd do that to us!

EVA: Tell us his problems like that!

JAMES: How could he ...

(Eva starts to gag and choke.)

EVA: He has ... Oh ... my car ... Ohmycar ...

JAMES: Neeeerrrggg ... I'm so mad and so guilty ... I can't see straight.

(They both collapse to the ground. Madison is awestruck.)

EVA: Could everyone gather around. I know this is a stressful situation but its important we ... remain ... remain ... Everyone! EveryONE! ONE. ONE. Every ... Please! PLEAse. REmain calm. Calm. I know this is a stressful—CAL—situation but we ... all of—Everyone please—need to remain CALM. Garther ... gather. We can't let these things just get to us. We need some perspective and to put these things into the proper context. We have to control ourselves OKAY?

OKAY!!? We CAN'T let them make us tear each other apart like wolves. EVER! Horrible, HORRIBLE violent wolves. With their teeth ever so sharp and ripping each others skin off with their teeth ever so sharp and the ripping like THE. SOUND. LIKE. swiping a credit card …

(Eva stiffly mimics swiping a credit card repeatedly. James lets loose one long REALLY dramatic scream. A spotlight falls onto Eva, who looks up emptily.)

VOICE: Eva Brea!

EVA: I'm a police … officer.

VOICE: Your car has finished inspection.

(Everyone stares up towards the light. TENSION!)

VOICE: Your car has … passed.

EVA: Ha … Ha …

(Eva smiles. She's dazed. The spotlight fades and she looks around, almost about to cry.)

EVA: I—I—

JAMES: You don't have to say anything …

(The Man with the Nice Collared Shirt enters.)

MAN IN A NICE COLLARED SHIRT: Ms. Brea? Congratulations. If you could sign here and your sticker is already on your car.

(Eva signs the clipboard. James looks on.)

JAMES: Eva … uh … I want to tell yo—

(Eva, not paying attention, exits. James stares off. He swallows his pride.)

JAMES: Never mind. *(Looks at the Man.)* Women, huh?

(The Man with the Nice Collared Shirt looks at him strangely.)

MAN IN A NICE COLLARED SHIRT: Yes … Women.

(The Man begins to write on the clipboard. Madison turns to Hannah.)

MADISON: Listen, uh, I don't normally do this but can I get your number? Maybe we could meet up, get some coffee, you could beat the shit out of me if you wanted …

HANNAH: No.

MADISON: We could just get coffee.

HANNAH: I'm sorry. I don't know you.

MADISON: I guess that's the point of the coffee. You know, to get to know each other—

EVA *(O.S.)*: MY SANDWICH!!!

(Eva runs back onstage.)

EVA: FUCKING PIECE OF SHIT! YOU TOUCHED MY STUFF! YOU TOUCHED ALL OF MY STUFF!

(Eva throws the Man onto the ground and begins to strangle him.)

EVA: Fuck you! Fuck you! Fuck you! I'm going to kill you, you understand me? I'm going to fucking kill you, you sonuvabitch!

(Everyone stares, shocked as Eva strangles the Man. Madison and Hannah look horrified but afraid to interfere. James just stares.)

MADISON: Stop!

EVA: Fuck you!

(Madison takes a step forward and Eva pulls the gun and points it at him. Eva cocks the gun and is about to point it at The Man when the Man pulls the tazer out and gives Eva a shock. She collapses to the ground and shakes. The Man gets to his feet, fixes his collar, and stares down at the out-of-commission Eva. He picks up his clipboard, makes some notes, and exits. James looks at Eva for a while, then gets up and stares off nervously, picking at his nails as he had in the beginning. Hannah turns to Madison.)

HANNAH: What were you saying?

MADISON: I was just talking about getting to know … Never mind.

HANNAH: That's a nice bag.

MADISON: Yeah. I had it custom made.

HANNAH: Oh yeah?

MADISON: Yeah, some guy in Italy did it.

HANNAH: What's it for? Money?

MADISON: Yeah.

HANNAH: Oh, cool.

MADISON: Yeah, it is.

(Hannah puts on her headphones. Madison holds his moneybag. James picks his nails. Eva shakes. Everyone is nervous.)

(Blackout)

(End of play.)

The Best Plays From The Strawberry One-Act Festival— Volume Five
Compiled by Van Dirk Fisher

SYNOPSIS OF PLAYS

COLD APRIL by John P. McEneny. Set in Rawanda in 1994, a thirteen-year old girl refuses to hand over her friends to the Hutu rebels.

REUNION by Brian Podnos. A father and son must face their demons when the son is released from rehab.

FIGHTING FIRES by Von H. Washington, Sr. On the eve of his 18th birthday, a young man kidnaps his absentee father and demands the attention he believes was owed him during his developmental years.

JACK by Daren Taylor. In a world where poverty and despair are in abundance, what happens when a boy buys magic seeds from a mysterious figure, climbs an enchanted beanstalk, and believes that he's seen God? Jack, a dark retelling of an old fairy tale. For every dream, there's a nightmare.

MARKED by Cassandra Lewis, a dark comedy that explores the connection between love, insanity and social responsibility.

ALWAYS ANASTASIA by Michele Leigh. A disillusioned cop on the verge of a nervous breakdown believes he is being tormented by a narcissistic psychopath.

THIS QUIET HOUSE by Toby Levin. What happens when a stepmother's desire to have a son catches fire?

WHAT CHEER, IOWA by Jeff Belanger. Tempers flare and sanity is on the line as five people struggle against the gargantuan pressure of waiting to find out if their cars passed their annual inspection.

ABOUT THE AUTHOR

Van Dirk Fisher

Van Dirk Fisher is the Artistic Director of the Riant Theatre and a graduate of the High School of Performing Arts in New York City and S.U.N.Y. at Purchase. He has produced *The Strawberry One-Act Festival, My Soul Sings Too, Sister; A Play Festival Celebrating The Spirit of Women, The International Lesbian & Gay Theatre Festival*, directed and written several musicals including: *Somebody's Calling My Name, Sweet Blessings, Tracks, Loving That Man Of Mine, Rock-A My Soul In The Bosom Of Abraham* and *Revelations*. Plays include: *A Special Gift, A Sin Between Friends, The Banjo Lesson, Mixed Blessings, Hotel Paradise* and *The Atlanta Affair*. Realty Show: *Who's Got Game?* An improvisational show in which 20 actors compete for the title of Best Playa Playa and a cash prize. The show can be seen on Riant TV (RTV) at www.therianttheatre.com/video.

Mr. Fisher is the author of *LOVING YOU, The Novel.*

Everyone wants a soul mate.
The hardest part is choosing between your heart and soul.

They said there would be no secrets between them. And there weren't. She just didn't tell Michael her lover's name. It wasn't important anyway, not now, because after today, she would never see Justin again.

Justin was preoccupied with Mariah as they stepped outside so he didn't notice the gray BMW parked across the street. He should have been paying attention, but he wasn't. All he could think about was Mariah. She loved him, and he knew it. She just didn't want to admit it, but he knew it. The CD by Darnerien was one clue. The fact that she didn't keep any photos of Michael on her desk was another. Oh yeah, Justin was full of himself. He thought he had Mariah pegged, but what he didn't know was that she kept Michael's picture closer than her desk. In fact, she wore his picture in a locket that she wore around her neck. Michael was the closest to her heart. Closest to the warmest part of her body that left her moist at night when she lay in bed alone thinking about him long after he had gone. Yes, Mariah was fortunate. She was loved by two men.

Available online at www.therianttheatre.com, www.barnesandnoble.com and www.amazon.com

To order the soundtrack to LOVING YOU go to www.therianttheatre.com. You can hear the soundtrack at www.myspace.com/lovingyouthemusical

Printed in the United States
205725BV00001B/88-99/P

9 780595 513239